By My Vampire Tonight
A Darklander series, Book 1
By Renee Field

Be My Vampire Tonight

Darklander Lovers

Renee Field

Published by Renee Field, 2018.

BE MY VAMPIRE TONIGHT

First edition. February 11, 2018.

ISBN: 978-1393206521

Written by Renee Field.

Chapter One

"You need to wiggle your ass more."

Mitch glared at Hank. *Only a werecat would say that.* "I am not wiggling my ass."

Hank strutted forward, hands on his waist in a masculine pose while sashaying his hips to showcase his point. He pivoted and cast a knowing wink at Mitch.

"Not bad," said Lance, teasing Mitch.

Mitch barreled in on him in a move that had Lance immediately taking a step back. "You're a bloody warlock. You don't need to wiggle your ass, you can just cast a spell on some unsuspecting woman." Mitch tugged on the black tuxedo. The collar was tight and he felt constricted in the formal suit.

"Stop fidgeting. You look great...for a man who's over a century old," said Sasha, pushing them into the herd of other men who were participating in the Darklander blind date charity auction.

"I am not old," snarled Mitch. He yanked on the tape holding his number, twenty-two, which was strapped to his suit jacket arm and once again had to resist the urge to rip it off and run for his freedom.

Sasha's hand ever so lightly rested on his arm. "Yes you are my dear, but like good wine, you age gracefully."

Mitch let her get away with her teasing. She was like a baby sister to him and he'd do anything for her.

Hank straightened his shoulders. "She's right, you are old."

Lance, wearing number twenty-three, glanced at Mitch. "Is that a gray hair I see?"

"Boys, behave," snapped Sasha, "Or I will turn you all into toads."

"I'd love to see you try that," taunted Lance.

"Brother dear, you have a very short memory...I turned you into a lizard last year."

Mitch shared a look of commiseration with Hank, who was yanking on the taped number, twenty-one, which was double-taped to his arm. Both of them broke into laughter.

"And I turned you into a ladybug, sister dear," replied Lance.

Mitch knew they could banter back and forth all evening, but if he was seriously going to go through with this the time was now. "Sasha if you want me to strut my stuff it's now or never. Personally, I'd take never any day."

"Trust me you won't regret it," said Sasha. Once again she ushered them into their proper order and marched them up to the side entrance of the stage.

Hank leaned in closer to Mitch. "Trust me, wiggling your ass will work."

With those parting words Mitch found himself front and center on the dark stage that was backlit with red lights. Hands on his hips, he fell into stride behind his buddies. He couldn't believe he'd been talked into participating in this Darklander-human farce.

Five years ago this would have been impossible for him and his buddies. In the span of half a decade the Darklander creatures, beings like himself—vampires, werecats and werewolves, fairies, genies and magical creatures—were let loose in the human realm. All thanks to a private peace treaty signed by the Secretary of the United Nations and the Mistress of the Darklander Council, who had ruled the council for the past two hundred years. Thanks to the Mistress' efforts the Darklander inhabitants, beings that existed since the beginning of Earth's fledgling years, were now able to live amongst the humans as long as they didn't disclose "what" they truly were. *A small price to pay for being able to jostle with humans,* thought Mitch, who had at one time been *just* that.

"Don't forget to smile, but no fangs," warned Sasha.

Mitch grinned at her, ensuring she saw all his fangs. She playfully slapped him on the shoulder.

"Behave, Mitch...you'll get your fun later tonight."

Mitch arched an eyebrow at her. As a powerful witch, Sasha was a force to be reckoned with, plus she was Lance's sister and he thought of her like a sibling. That was the only reason he'd agreed to strut his stuff on stage like some human playboy. Sasha loved the theater.

A year ago she'd acquired it to help those Darklander beings adjust to the strange yet exhilarating human world. The theater provided the stage for beings like himself to unleash their wild sides. It had become in a short amount of time a safe haven for Darklander who found it hard to adjust to the constraints of the human world. Why? Because it was hard to remember the law the United Nations had imposed on them. No human could discover they existed. Being written about through folklore, fairy tales and even in romance books was safe but having your true identity broadcast loud and clear on the television was a big no-no.

A shiver of cold dread caused Mitch's gut to clench uneasily. Sasha was also a huge mischief maker and something told him that besides strutting his stuff his life was about to change. *Change isn't always a good thing.* A vision of the deal he'd agreed to more than a century ago with Lucifer, the god of hell, blazed hot and terrifying through his mind.

"You're on boys! Strut your stuff and make all those women scream for more."

Saved from painful memories, Mitch followed after his buddies. At six foot six, Hank, the werecat, fought his inner beast on a daily basis just like Mitch. Five years ago, Mitch, a vampire, had learned how to slip into human society by working as a cop on the nightshift. After almost a century living in the Darklander realm he'd given up hope of ever finding his perfect mate.

Lance, his warlock buddy, couldn't use his magical skills in the day but come night he could play all he wanted. Generations ago a curse leveled at Lance's family had made the warlocks non-magical during the day, so slipping into the human realm seemed like an easy adjustment for him. However, Mitch knew that Lance thirsted for revenge on the witch family that made him basically useless when the sun was out. He totally understood that. *We're all damned.*

In his one hundred and twenty years as a vampire Mitch had never done anything remotely like this. Part of him thought it was crude while his baser macho instinct automatically preened before the crowd of oohing and ahhing women who were madly raising their hands shouting out his number.

"They like you," taunted Lance.

Mitch didn't say anything. He lengthened his stride to ensure he almost floated behind Hank and then did a slow turn just like his werecat friend. Then he flexed his forearms moving them to rest behind his head in a casual pose following another copycat move like Hank, and decided he'd finally gone barking mad.

It was then her scent snagged him. Hot, lust-filled blood, ripe for the taking. More than that, he felt her mind push. That tingling awareness that said the woman, filled with thoughts of sex, was a psychic—a powerful one at that. He turned, his gaze catching on the long chestnut mane of curls streaked with hues of auburn and corn yellow colors noting how it trailed past her pale bare, shoulders. She shuddered, completely aware of his want.

For the first time in years Mitch's cock hardened with mind-blowing lust pouring like thick, warm blood through his veins. Physically he had to resist the urge to leap off the stage, grab the woman who had attracted his attention and bite into her vein, taking her precious desire-inducing lifeforce. The sensation was so strong Mitch's cock and his balls tightened, the need for release a hot pulsing beacon that said she was his. Take her. Claim her. To hell with the consequences. And there would be consequences because she was blasted human.

Another mind push from her caused his steps to falter. She was basically telling him to back off. He growled, the sound a low vibration laced with dangerous intent. *I don't think so. Mine. You. Are. Mine. You just don't know it yet. But tonight you will.*

For the first time that evening Mitch truly grinned, ensuring no fangs revealed themselves. With his cock rock hard for the tantalizing taste of O-negative blood he couldn't wait to escape the theater and get his just reward for the night.

When the endless marching around the stage ceased and they were finally able to exit, Sasha rushed up to them.

"Thank you...thank you. You guys were a huge hit. I just knew it."

"For you only, Sasha," said Mitch, giving her an elegant old-fashioned bow.

Sasha gaily chuckled like she had as a child when he used to bow to her to teach her how to do a proper lady's curtsy. Those lessons more than often gave them both a serious case of the giggles. Over the years, Mitch had come to realize Sasha only learned things when it suited her and not the other way around. Kind-hearted almost to a fault, she was all lady even if she never did learn the proper way to curtsy.

Shoving an envelope and red rose into Mitch's hand, Sasha continued. "Okay here, this is your date, Mitch. And yes, it's the one you want. The instructions are outlined in the letter. This is for you Hank," she handed the werecat a tiger lily flower and envelope. "And voila, brother dear." Sasha held a yellow daisy out for Lance with a similar envelope. "Be nice. They paid a small fortune for you and don't forget this is a date. Have fun. See you tomorrow night."

All three men groaned loudly but it was Mitch's growl that tugged a smile from Sasha's retreating form.

"I got him. Number twenty-one!" squealed Nora.

"That's only because you outbid me," snapped Cindy. "Anyway, it doesn't matter I've got the one I really wanted. Number twenty-three. Who did you get, Tina?"

Tina gulped. "I think I got number twenty-two but that's not who I wanted. I was trying to bid for the guy across from him...number thirty-three."

"Twenty-two...wasn't that the spooky one?" asked Cindy.

"Wasn't that the guy who looked like he was floating on the stage?" asked Nora. "It doesn't matter. It's just a date, don't worry about it."

"Yeah, it's a date...you do remember what that is, *right*?" teased Cindy.

Tina took another drink of the pink liquor her friends had bought her. She twirled the tiny matching fuchsia umbrella with her fingers. Before she could say anything a beautiful woman with long straight black hair wearing a gorgeous short black dress approached the table. The only thing out of place was the bold purple witch's hat she wore. Then again this was a theater charity auction and all the money was going toward the construction of the new theater playhouse next door.

"Ladies, I'm Madam Sasha. I can't thank you enough for your generous bids. Here are your envelopes. The men you each picked are very, very special.

"Just how special?" Cindy grinned, giving the woman a bold wink.

"You will not be disappointed."

"Actually, I was trying to bid on thirty-three." Tina seriously hoped to rearrange her date. While there was nothing wrong with the gorgeous man decked out in the kill-me now tuxedo, his haunting good looks and deep chocolate brown eyes had evoked a dangerous twittering in her she felt straight from her hot core to her curled toes.

Madam Sasha pinned her with an intense stare. "Thirty-three will not fulfill you. Trust me, it's twenty-two you really need. And as much as he might be gruff and all macho-like, just keep in mind that one is never too old to learn new tricks."

"Tricks?" asked Tina, clearly confused.

"Yes, tricks," snickered her friends in unison.

Tina shushed them. *Why did I agree to this?* Tina thought there was a lot left unsaid by the woman's cryptic remark but she had vowed to have fun, and let her hair down and that's exactly what she was going to do. *Maybe another drink would be a good idea.*

The woman reached out and placed a calming hand on Tina's bare shoulder. "Trust me. He will not disappoint."

Giving a somewhat committed smile, Tina nodded.

As if the woman had read her mind, she motioned for a passing waiter to bring a round of complimentary drinks to the table.

"This is going to be fun," sighed Nora.

"Yours is like a great, big pussycat and yours," the woman turned to look at Cindy, "He likes to think he knows it all but you're just the right woman to set him straight."

Cindy smiled but Tina had known her since university when all three were roommates. She knew her friend was trying to figure out if what Madam Sasha said was good news or bad.

"You know the rules ladies. The men will remain masked for your date. I must be off. You have one hour each to rendezvous with your men of the evening. Enjoy the night, ladies."

Tina took a sip of her drink. "Now, that was weird."

"She's just being theatric. This is a charity function for the theater playhouse," reminded Nora. "I don't care. I'm doing exactly what we planned to do. I'm having fun tonight. Salutations."

With their traditional salute they all took a long swig from their drinks, downing them in quick succession. Feeling slightly tipsy, Tina opened her envelope and grimaced. "Oh my god. I'm supposed to meet him at Dimitri's Restaurant but that's on the other side of town. I'll never make it."

"You will if you leave now and I would if I were you...twenty-two didn't appear to be the type of guy who likes to be left waiting."

With sweat breaking out on her skin, Tina realized the truth of Cindy's words. "Wish me luck," she said, reaching for her purse.

"You, my dear are not driving." Nora, the mother hen's harsh words of warning broke into Tina's thoughts.

"How many drinks did you have?" asked Cindy.

Tina closed her eyes and counted. They all had one drink at her house before leaving for the night, then another when they arrived at the charity auction and two more since then. "You're right. I can't drive. I'll just call a cab."

"Tina dear, you have a driver. Just call him," said Cindy, reminding her that she still wasn't comfortable with her newfound wealth.

"But I didn't ask him."

Both friends leaned their elbows on the black-draped tablecloth. "He's your employee...your driver. That's what he's supposed to do," stated Cindy in her I-told-you-so voice.

Nodding at her, Nora said, "Call him."

"Fine," said Tina, rolling her eyes at her friends. She hit speed dial on her cell phone and within seconds felt more relaxed.

"He'll be here in ten minutes. He asked if either of you need a lift anywhere."

Sorting through her own purse, Nora mumbled. "Thanks, but I've got my own wheels." She ripped open her own envelope. "Damn!"

"What?"

"I'm just going to walk. My date's at Cara's Lounge and that's only two blocks from here. Where's yours, Cindy?"

Both Tina and Nora watched Cindy slowly peel the envelope open. "Oh," she said.

Reaching for her shawl, Tina teased. "Oh, is that a restaurant?"

"Not funny. My date's at Finn's."

"Finn's? But you can't go up there, you're afraid of heights. Can we trade?" asked Tina, hopefully.

"Not on your life. I bid on him and he's mine. If I don't look down I'll be okay," replied Cindy, grabbing her leather jacket, her face already chalky white.

"Cindy, you do realize that Finn's is outside and on top of the highest building in the city, right?" said Nora.

Cindy stood up, hooking her purse over her shoulder. "Cut that out. I can do this."

Tina watched her friend belt her coat tightly and walk with pride out of the theater's hall that was adjacent to the main theater currently under reconstruction. "You shouldn't tease her about her problem with heights," she said, chastising Nora.

"If I tease her about her height issue she won't think too much about the guy she's about to date. We're all alike. Cindy is all work and no play. I honestly can't remember the last time she went out on a date. And, you're thirty-one, still a virgin and still trying to squirm out of your own date. Tina, this is exactly what you need. Relax, have some fun and let that wild woman out to play."

"Wild woman...you can't be serious." Tina chuckled to herself.

"Well, if you're not, I know I'm certainly going to be wild and wicked. It's about time we all had some serious fun."

"Isn't serious fun an oxymoron?"

"See, that's exactly what I mean. No more big words."

"Okay no more big words. Let's just be wild and free and let the night shake our skin."

Nora draped her arm around her, hugging Tina close. "Now that's my girl. See, there is a poet in you after all...once you banish the lawyer you've become."

"Hey, I like being a lawyer."

"Yeah, and I like being the mother hen and Cindy likes being the cold, corporate climbing bitch, too. Our labels suck."

Stifling giggles, the two of them sauntered unsteadily toward the exit. Once outside the cool of the night breeze sailed into Tina, causing her to shiver. "You sure you want to walk?"

"Yeah, I like the outdoors. It's only two blocks. Don't worry, I'm carrying my kill-them-in-the-eye mace in my purse." Nora giggled and then whistled. "Nice car."

Tina felt her cheeks turn bright red. "I don't think I'm ever going to get used to this."

"It's only been a few months, Tina. Give yourself time, you'll adjust to your new wealth. Have fun. No. I take that back. Have lots and lots of fun."

Giving a final wave to Nora, Tina climbed into the sleek white limousine.

"Dimitri's Restaurant, Ma'am?" asked the driver, clarifying her earlier instructions.

"Yes, thank you."

"My pleasure, Ma'am."

Before Tina could remind him that she hated that title, her driver automatically slid the black window up, cutting her off. Tina trailed her hands along the cool feel of the black leather seats and marveled once again all this was hers. Closing her eyes, she let herself be driven to her rendezvous of the night, determined to have fun, play it wild and if possible force the man to take her virginity.

That idea she hadn't shared with her friends. Tonight Tina was feeling desperate. *Surely to god, I can tempt one man into my bed.*

"We are here, Ma'am." The driver slid the window down while maneuvering the car to Dimitri's entrance.

She stepped out of the limousine as her driver held the door open. "Thank you."

"Will I be picking you up?"

"Ahh..." Tina mumbled, casting a look to the sidewalk. "I'll call you."

"I am at your disposal." With those words her driver gave an old-fashioned bow and climbed back into the driver's side. A minute later the limo was out of sight.

Thirty minutes later Tina was fuming mad. Her date, the man she had bid a thousand dollars on, had left a note with the head waiter stating something had come up and he'd make amends by showing up at her place tonight precisely at midnight.

The nerve! Whipping her cell phone out she punched speed dial, again, angry at her mystery date who dared to be a no-show. *He doesn't even know where I live so how the hell can he show up at my door at midnight? What a lying bastard.*

"Home, please" said Tina, climbing morosely back inside the limo feeling very much cheated out of her wild, wicked night.

Chapter Two

A moment of fear snaked straight to Tina's toes. The doorbell chimed a second time, the soft twittering of the bird sounds startlingly cheery and bright. Two things she was not. It was midnight. Actually it was two minutes past midnight and her blind date had mysteriously found her house and shown up. Tina was pleased she had dared to hope he'd follow through and even happier she'd dressed for seduction.

She dragged in a much needed breath and marshaled her thoughts. *It's now or never.* Lurching forward she yanked open the door. Instantly a hot, heavy feeling invaded her. Panic seized her and the urge to slam the door shut before she did something she'd regret all her life caused her to freeze.

"May I come in?"

The man's voice was soft yet it rumbled with an odd sense of familiarity tugging at every feminine cell within her body. Expensive aged whiskey, Cuban cigars and leather. Three uniquely masculine scents clogged the doorway to her house, wafting in to invade her womanly senses like a pistol firing. She came alive. All hot and bothered with a want of need. Tina forced herself to swallow. Normally that was an easy thing to do, but not tonight. She was parched, her body yearned to bend toward his wickedly dark aroma that said man, lust and sex. Tonight though, it was her turn to sample a piece of the decadent for a change.

Not trusting herself to speak, she nodded and moved away from the door, allowing the mystery man to enter her domain. He shut the door behind him and locked it.

Hugging herself, a shiver of delicious delight traveled through her mind and now achy body. Tina was an even five feet. The man dwarfed her—a good six footer, built like a quarterback, all solid muscle, yet agile on his feet as he strolled into her house. Round shoulders and muscular arms hugged the black formal suit he wore. The Zorro-like mask reaffirmed he was her blind date from the auction.

The realization of what she was hoping *this* man would do to her tonight caused panic to blaze in every rational part of her mind. The truth that after tonight she'd no longer be a virgin caused her to shut her eyes.

"It's okay if you want me to go. I'll understand."

"What?" Her eyes flashed open, clearly surprised by his statement.

"You were looking for someone else."

"No, I wasn't. Well, actually," she giggled. "No. I mean you'll do. Oh my god I can't believe I just said that. I'm sorry, that didn't come out like I meant it to. And I'm rambling." Tina sucked in a shuddering breath. "I'm not sure what I'm supposed to do." She pulled the pink silk bathrobe around her body tighter, unconsciously tying the tie in a double knot.

"You look beautiful." He took a step toward her. "And you don't need to do anything except let *me* pleasure you."

His voice was commanding...full of dark, erotic promises...lush, hot intent.

"Are you sure? I mean if you want to go, I'll understand. I'm not really beautiful. You're just saying that."

The man moved in on her space, walking with a fluid glide making it appear as if he were floating toward where she stood with one hand holding the banister, still anchoring her in place. Without hesitating he cupped her face in one large hand. She inhaled the smell of his male cologne, identifying it instantly as Axe. Immediately it conjured images of locker rooms full of naked muscular men. Tina knew instantly this man was the one she wanted.

Okay, I guess I got the right one after all.

Holding on to your virginity for Mr. Right was so outdated her own mother, the same woman who had adopted her when she was an infant, had begged her to get laid. It had been a very telling conversation to have with her mother, a year before she was killed in a car wreck. It had also been sad, because her mother believed in living life to the fullest and that was something Tina wanted.

Now here she was, thirty-one and still a virgin. Just once Tina wanted to know exactly what it felt like and if she couldn't get Mr. Right, well she'd get the next best thing—a man who would fulfill her fantasy and give her mind-blowing sex. So what if she'd never see him again. So what if she couldn't see his entire face or know his name. At least she'd get what she wanted.

"I'm going to kiss you," he said, a moment before his head dipped down and his lips gently tugged at her own. She felt a small nip on her lower lip. His tongue darted out to tease the bite. The movement was blatantly erotic. Her eyelids closed as she gave into the dark promise of fulfillment this man was rewarding her with.

Within seconds his tender explorations evoked a passionate response within her. She attempted to place her hands around his large frame but he was too tall for her to twine her arms around his neck. Tina opened her mouth wider, allowing his probing tongue to delve deep. His hands skimmed in a reassuring seductive leisurely stroke down her back, the silky material of her bathrobe a reminder she had dressed for the occasion. Underneath the robe, she wore matching bright pink panties and bra.

"Is your bedroom upstairs?"

"Yes."

He didn't hesitate to scoop her up into his arms. She felt strangely enamored being cocooned next to his solid frame while being cradled in his muscular arms. At the top of the stairs, she said, "To your right." She noted his eyes taking in all the bedrooms on the top level.

"I know."

"You do?" Her mind immediately opened up to his, instinct taking over as she scanned him. Nothing. He was closed to her. A shiver of dread and excitement, of knowing she couldn't control him, fluttered to life.

He smiled, the grin knowing and sinfully dark.

"This is a big house for one person."

"Don't I know it. I inherited it from my father."

"Must cost a fortune to heat."

His teasing smile caused nervous butterflies to fly in circles in her belly and a pool of warm cream to seep from her cunt.

"Let's make sure you don't need to turn that furnace on tonight."

She giggled into his chest. He grinned in earnest, his chocolate brown eyes heated to a darker shade. Tina went to point out which bedroom to enter but he stepped into the right one a moment before she could tell him.

"Now this I like." Immediately he strolled straight to the large King-sized bed. The bedroom decor was designed for seduction. Dark blood red walls, a rich navy blue comforter, and a roaring fireplace in the middle. This was the bedroom her friends called the sex room. The black velvet drapes added to the ensemble, all but screaming hot, sweaty sex.

Tina slid out of his arms, reluctantly. The minute her feet touched the plush carpet second thoughts surfaced. *Can I really do this?*

Reading the hesitation in her eyes and body language the man nudged her, causing the back of her knees to hit the bed. Gently he lowered her body to the bed, immediately claiming the space next to her. He trailed tender kisses down her neck as one hand started to untie the pink sash of her robe. For one second Tina hesitated, feeling shivers of dread skim like the goose bumps of desire along her flesh. Then he spoke. The possessive words warming her further while eroding away at her doubt.

"I need you. You want me. You are mine."

His words stroked her mind, bending her will to his, sending all her inhibitions to scatter.

"I need to see all of you but you sure know how to tie a knot."

A second later the ties were ripped in half. A devilish sin-filled grin spread across his face and instantly Tina squirmed with a rush of desire as her cunt screamed at him to take her right now. Anywhere. Any way. The urge to climb onto his body and take control rocked through her, shaking her rational mind and soul. She attempted to clutch her robe together with her hands.

His large hands moved hers, placing her arms by her side. Painstakingly slow he opened the robe, unwrapping her with a sense of awe warming her thundering heart. She squeezed her eyes shut the minute the cool air of the room touched her skin, and flashed them open when a guttural groan tore from him.

"You are so beautiful. Like an angel."

The nonsense words flattered and helped to reassure her it was going to be okay. But his mouth, the minute it reverently fastened onto one of her puckered nipples that was straining against the satiny bra she still wore, said to hell with second thoughts.

"Like a fat angel," she automatically said.

"Fat? Sweet-cakes I don't know what idiot said you were fat but let me tell you they were dead wrong...or deserve to be dead. There is nothing more appealing than a woman with curves. I'm the type of man who likes to sink his hands and teeth into something deliciously hot. And I can't wait to sink them into you."

He followed his words with action. Unclasping the front of her bra he removed it off her arms within seconds, taking the choice completely away from her. *This is exactly what I needed.*

Then his tongue licked her large right breast, teasing the underside as he fondled it. He repeated the action with her other breast and then squeezed them together, merging his head into the valley he had created. He groaned, the rumble of his voice and hot breath on her sensitive skin causing a wet trickle of desire to seep onto her panties.

It was his heart-felt confession that sent all her inhibitions that were screaming she was doing the wrong thing out the window. To hear a man say he liked her curves, instead of telling her in a coy manner she might want to get a membership to a gym, endeared this nameless man to her.

What he was doing to her breasts had a direct pull on her stomach muscles. *Now if only Pilates could do this for me, I'd have a flat tummy within weeks.* Tina stifled a giggle when he moved his head from her breasts to tweak each nipple, causing both to become achy, pointy and flush dark brown.

However she stilled when his hand moved to rest on her mound, and her breath hitched as he slowly pushed a hand inside her panties.

"Relax. I'm not going to hurt you." His reassuring and commanding voice was all the encouragement she needed. She arched into his caress.

His fingers delved through her now-drenched pussy curls and she thoroughly enjoyed his tender explorations. The rough feel of his fingers on her now-swollen pussy lips caused her to squirm with unbridled desire. This was a man who used his hands. This was also a man who knew exactly what to do with his fingers to entice a woman to come to that blessed brink of sexual ecstasy within seconds.

"So fucking wet. You're unbelievable."

"Thank you." She breathed the word out. "Could you please take off your clothes?"

He chuckled, the hot feel of his laugh causing goose bumps to flare once again to life all over her now ultra-sensitive body.

"Yeah, I think I can manage that."

The loss of his hot, manly body from her skin was immediately apparent. It left her feeling bereft and shaky. The urge to drag his masculine frame back onto hers like a wanton woman slammed into her.

Where did my common sense go? And just when did I become a lush in the bedroom? Those two thoughts squirmed into her consciousness but she quickly shut off her rational mind. If she didn't do that she'd scamper off the bed and flee her own house, and that wouldn't do. She was the one who had asked for this. She was the one insisting Cindy, Nora and herself should all go have some wild, wicked fun at the theater's blind date charity auction. There was no way she was going to back out now.

Not when heaven was within reach. Not when she'd finally discover what all the fuss was about sex. *No way am I not getting satisfied tonight. This man wants me.*

Taking a daring breath, Tina moved to her elbows to watch him. First he discarded his tuxedo jacket then he undid the buttons of his white dress shirt, parting it to reveal a muscular, dark hairy chest. Her fingers itched to tease his chest hairs and her tongue longed to lick his nipples. With his hands on his pants he stared intently at her.

"Are you one hundred percent sure about this?"

Tina licked her parched lips and nodded.

"Well, I do aim to please." A moment later he stepped out of his dress pants, revealing he was commando.

A gasp tore from Tina's lips a second before she could help it.

"Not to your liking?" He placed his hands on his hips in a very GQ pose. The action caused his cock to jut out, teasing her with its manly stance. This man was proud and unabashed in his skin, which was more than Tina could say for how she felt about herself.

"Ahh, no, it's just that I've never seen a naked man before," she blurted out.

"You're kidding, right?" He sounded gruff to her ears and slightly pissed off.

"No. I'm not kidding. Raised Catholic." She rolled her eyes for good measure.

"I didn't see any crosses."

"My adopted mother raised me Catholic but I'm not a true believer."

"Good for me," he grinned. "But surely you looked at a magazine or something with your girl friends?"

"No, couldn't do it. I wanted to but...I mean I thought it would be with...ahh, never mind."

She watched the man with the melted dark chocolate eyes assess her. His muscular chest was covered with the perfect amount of dark, curly hair as he loomed over her. Tina especially loved the swatch of hair that trailed a teasing line below his bellybutton. Her eyes were drawn to his thick mat of hair nestled above his large cock.

He placed both arms over her body, holding himself rigidly in place over her, on top, but not touching. Even still she felt his heat—that totally intoxicating masculine scent of him that reminded her of hard, worn leather and whiskey.

"You honor me with being the first man to please you."

Still towering over her, he dragged her bottom lip into his mouth and suckled. The move was sultry and seductive and timed to give her pause. She knew he was a real gentleman right then and there.

"There's no going back if I let my body touch yours." His voice had lowered and it was filled with sexual longing.

"Please. Please continue," she mumbled into his mouth.

"Do you want to know what I'm going to do to you?"

She nodded, arching her head up to better meet his lips that were still teasing her own while he talked.

"I'm going to suckle your breasts until you're so wet for my cock that you'll want to scream. Then I'm going to part your thighs and eat you. I can't wait for that part. I'm going to lick that pussy of yours until you climax, your cum sliding down my throat and then and only then will I give you what you really need. Only then will I slide my cock into your unbelievably tight sheath. I'm going to take it slow, let you get used to the feel of my cock wedged deep within you before I pump it into you like I know you'll want. And then I'm going to claim you. I will mark you as mine. Your blood will be mine and you will crave me...need me...want me. Am I clear?"

"Oh. My. God." Tina squirmed while her pussy muscles screamed their own hallelujah. He nuzzled an earlobe, causing her to twist and moan.

"Let's leave god out of this for tonight. It's all about you, Sweet-cakes. I'm your man."

Tina seriously wanted to say something but he moved from her earlobe to trail a hot path of kisses down her neck to her breasts and then he feasted on them.

Heaven! That was the word Tina would use to describe the incredible sensation of his mouth on her now-heaving breasts. Where before he had played with them, now he seriously worked them. He was a man of detailed precision. He took his time, like he was memorizing the feel of her nipples, what they liked and ached for. He'd blow a hot breath across the tip then draw it sinfully into his welcoming mouth, while his fingers played and tweaked her other nipple. The stimulation of his mouth and fingers on her breasts was too much for Tina.

The need for that elusive "more" hammered into her as she squirmed on top of the duvet cover. Blessedly, he moved his large body down hers, kissing her skin the entire way.

Tina didn't hesitate when he parted her thighs. On his knees in front of the bed, with his charcoal wavy brown hair he looked like a dark-edged Adonis, a man intent on pleasuring her mindlessly. She so wanted that...needed it.

She thought he'd go straight for her pussy. Instead he teased the insides of her thighs with small licks and nips, his tongue tasting the small bites that merged pain with pleasure, causing her to feel edgy.

"I can't take any more." She flung a hand over her eyes. The intense wash of pleasure crawling over her sensitive skin was almost too much for her.

"You can and you will." A second later he forked his tongue onto her swollen pussy lips, teasing them with a tender, soft lick. He repeated his stroke a dozen times, until she was once again raging in her head for him to really give her pussy a good licking.

Just when she thought she couldn't take another second of his slow sexual torture, his tongue delved deep, opening her cunt to move straight into her wet core. Then bliss and torture became one. Between his long strokes within her core and his sweep up to her pebbled achy clit she became a mindless, thrashing woman on the verge of her first orgasm. Her entire body was screaming for it. And then it happened. He nipped her clit hard, bringing that achy pointy bud into his mouth with a twirl of his tongue, causing her to instantly shatter. A gush of warm liquid escaped her body and Tina wished she could feel embarrassed over it. Instead an unbelievable, mind-shattering feeling of satisfaction roared through her bones. The sound of him licking her clean...the tenderness of his ministrations was heart wrenching, soothing and reassuring.

"So fucking sweet. You are unbelievable."

He kissed his way from her cunt to her own lips. The taste of her own tangy juices on his lips was a slight shock, the flavor salty and muskier than she would have thought. Instead of repelling her it awoke a raw hunger within her for more.

She felt his massive cock nudge against her parted legs, the head bouncing along on purpose. Then the tip of his shaft was poised at her entrance. He stilled, keeping it poised at her slick opening, making her delicious want him more. His mouth descended in one quick movement to claim her neck. She arched more into him, allowing his mouth to suckle the throbbing vein and then he bit her, hard, breaking through skin. Her body instantly stilled as pain laced through her, but then blistering warmth speared her body when he started to suckle her neck. Tina's toes curled and another shattering orgasm screamed its release, leaving her body totally satisfied and for once in her life her mind felt barrier-free.

No penetrating sounds of the everyday world crashed in to invade her consciousness. It was just him. His heat, his scent, his wants and needs stealing into her and she welcomed it all. The gift of silencing the rest of the world...of living truly in the moment, Tina grasped with all her might.

Her hands raked long marks down his back as she urged him on, the suckling sensation of his mouth pulling her stomach muscles, making her body squirm once again with desire.

Tina urged her legs around his, wishing he'd lower his body fully onto her. *This is it. Thank god.* She was finally going to be deflowered. The old-fashioned expression was a term Nora used. Her friend usually said it with a wide gleeful smile plastered to her face.

Then Tina heard it...a buzzing sound that was not coming from her blissful self. "What's that noise?" She prayed to the Almighty her doorbell wasn't acting up again.

"Aw, fuck. Excuse me a moment."

Incredulously, Tina watched the man pull out a cell phone from the pocket of his dress pants, which were lying on the floor by the bed. He flicked it open, looked at the number and then closed it, cursing in an unfamiliar language.

"I'm really sorry about this but I've got to go. Trust me, I don't want to." He sighed the last part of his sentence as a shaky hand tousled his hair.

Her blind date was dressed and out of the bedroom in seconds before Tina fully comprehended what his leaving truly meant.

No way. This is not happening to me. I won't let it happen.

Tina thrust her psychic mind at him, willing him to come back. The dark void of nothingness hit her hard. Then like butter warming in the hot noon sun she felt his touch. His stroke into her mind caused her nipples to pebble to tight buds. That one touch screamed she was his.

His possessiveness did not please her. *Wait a second. The blind date charity auction is on all week. First thing tomorrow morning I'm going to have a tête-à-tête with that Sasha person. I will get what I want. Being a lawyer is going to pay off for once.*

Tina yanked on her pink bathrobe and then walked down the stairs to ensure the speedy, sexy, tight-buns-of-steel man who had high-tailed it faster than lightning out of her bedroom hadn't forgotten to shut the front door in his haste to exit. The last thing she needed to deal with in the wee hours of the morning was a burglar. In the mood she was in she'd kill anyone with her bare hands. Explaining how she had become a deranged, sex-depraved lunatic to a judge was not an option.

Chapter Three

M itch Vlascenko was stone cold mad. First he was furious at himself for taking part in that ridiculous Darklander theater blind date auction. And secondly, he was sure Lucifer was laughing his ass off at him.

After one hundred and twenty years of being Lucifer's slave Mitch had thought he'd adjusted to the god of hell's dark demands. Giving up his human soul in a moment of weakness and striking a bargain with the Lord of the Damned wasn't an easy relationship at the best of times. With the new Darklander treaty allowing beings like himself to now live in the human realm, Lucifer's demands had only become stranger.

Nothing with Lucifer was ever as it seemed. Take for example the lure of the god of hell's tease he'd be happy, powerful, have everything he wanted and live for eternity if he willingly gave his human soul to him. Mitch's human life had been pitiful. He'd been a nobody and when the plague had ravaged through his Russian village he'd been one of the first to succumb.

He had at first thought the light he'd grasped onto had been heaven. When Lucifer offered him immortality, power and the means to enjoy life, Mitch hadn't objected. Letting the god of hell drain him of his blood, he'd willingly allowed Lucifer to change him. Pain the likes of which Mitch could still vividly recall had seized his body. When he'd awoken it was to discover he'd been banished from the human realm and sent to the Darklander realm. To say he had missed humankind would be an understatement. Thankfully, he'd made a few friends who understood his dilemma. When he'd asked Lucifer if there was a way he could gain his freedom the god of the hell told him servitude was for eternity until he found his true soulmate.

Like that was ever going to happen, he had thought.

Now it had. Every cell within his body recognized it. She—the human woman—was his soulmate. And Lucifer was demanding he claim her, the one woman in the universe who could bathe him in goodness, purity and light. The one woman who could grant him freedom. And he'd fled because the notion of letting Lucifer claim Tina didn't sit well with him.

He hadn't wanted to take the call but the minute he saw the number he knew he had to. If he didn't they'd both pay for it. A summons from Lucifer did not go unanswered.

Now, Mitch was fuming. Lucifer wanted him to claim Tina. His Tina. His mate. The urge to do so was a pounding blood-thirsty ache within him. When Mitch inhaled he could still smell her arousal, her sweet feminine perfume that was a soothing balm to his soul and an aphrodisiac to his cock.

Mitch, though, needed answers. Nothing was black and white when it came to dealing with the god of hell and the last thing Mitch wanted to do was make another person's life hell on earth.

The sun had set and it was now seven o'clock. Mitch was about to have his first day in a human court. *Too bad I'm not shaking in my boots.* A flashback to the Court of Death where Lucifer had sat as his judge, detailing his pathetic life triggered all his vampire instincts to surface. Back then though the god of hell had also painted a rosy picture of his new life if Mitch willingly handed over his soul. Once the bargain had been struck and the deal signed with blood, Mitch had entered his new life only to discover the Darklander realm—made up of shades of gray, was his new hell. Forced to learn how to cope with his new vampire abilities and need for blood, he'd also been forced to participate in the bloody civil war raging through the Darklander world. Creatures the likes he hadn't known existed warred with other magical beings. Mitch at first had thought he'd escaped the depravity of the plague on Earth, but forced to participate in the brutal factions battling for supremacy on the Darklander world was no better.

He choose his side and latched onto the fragile pact made up of other vampires, werewolves, and magical creatures like the fairies, witches and warlocks to side against the more explosive temperaments of the drákon, griffon and sidhe—the darker fairies who lived for chaos. When peace was finally claimed it took a decade to rebuild the Darklander world. Today it was equipped with majestic buildings made of glass that towered up through the gray skyline, and serene pools of clear white lakes with a variety of gray flowers that edged the border. There were still a few wild dark forests throughout the world but the treaty allowed for the drákon and the other beings to claim them as long as they didn't bother the civilized Darklander. What Mitch had missed the most in his new world was color. He lived year after year with shades of gray, white and black as backdrops for everything. So when finally a peace treaty was established between earth, Mitch hadn't hesitated to petition going home. Home to a world that existed in a vivid spectrum of colors. The pain to his senses those first days when he had to reacquaint color into his life had been Mitch's first lesson that what he'd given up for immortality might not have been worth it.

Mitch inhaled deeply, smelling that sweet, lust-filled innocent scent of Tina Abramova—the lawyer who was representing him tonight. The woman that was his. The same woman Lucifer wanted him to claim. Why Lucifer wanted that scared Mitch more than he cared to think about.

Mitch had often heard the other cops talk about Tina. Every unmarried cop and some married ones had the hots for her. Who wouldn't? She was petite in height and had that lush mane of coffee-colored textured hair with playful hues of auburn and blonde that cascaded down her back in a wave of desire, immediately causing a man to think about the silky feel of her strands on his skin. She was curvy in all the right places. A spectacular heart-shaped ass his hands fit perfectly around and bouncy breasts which caused a man to salivate with need. When Tina giggled that utterly feminine sound all eyes pinned her.

Worse, Mitch had discovered Tina was oblivious to it all. She kept her eyes downcast while clutching her brown no-nonsense briefcase tight against her chest. When forced to talk with one of the guys in blue she almost always stuttered. It was a strange trait for a strong psychic to develop.

A few of the guys were openly laughing that a man in uniform made her nervous. Mitch cast a dead glance their way. They wisely shut up and backed out of his sight. No one laughed at his Tina. No one. But someone was obviously laughing at him.

Mitch shook his head, hating his body was still hard and full of lust for Tina. He'd known the minute she had answered the door in that colorful silky pink outfit, welcoming him into her house that he was in deep shit. The woman had been slightly afraid of him. Wisely so.

She wanted a nice, gentle lover, not a man scarred by his past or fearful of getting too emotionally attached.

What woman pays for a man at a blind date charity auction in the hopes that he'll take her virginity? Mitch was pissed at himself. He was the type of man who would have willingly done that. *No strings attached. No emotion. No care. Heck, she doesn't even need to pay me. Talk about a great experience for a woman like Tina. She deserves better. Much better than me.*

His cell phone buzzed again. He groaned loudly. People took one look at him and quickly averted their gaze. To get a summons from Lucifer twice in twenty-four hours was not to his liking at all.

Mitch flipped it open. "I'm busy, what the hell do you want?"

The bitter laugh on the other end of the phone caused him to flinch.

BE MY VAMPIRE TONIGHT

TINA IGNORED HER CELL phone buzzing on her waist. Hooked onto her black dress skirt, she knew exactly who was calling her—her friends and some unknown number. Cindy had been the first to call promptly early in the morning and then Nora had called thirty minutes later. She'd ignored the calls then and would for the remainder of the day. The urge though to call her friends was pressing but before she could do that she had to get her story straight. There was no way she was seriously going to tell them what had happened.

The guy bailed on me. He fled the scene. Ohh, that's so charming. My blind date had other plans. Talk about letting the wild side out. Tina was angrier than she'd ever been in her life and she had a feeling that most of her clients and the few cops that had passed her way this morning sensed her mood. Most had backed away. Not all, but most.

She gripped her café latté tighter as she marched to the Clerk's office. Clutched in her other hand was an envelope she needed couriered ASAP. The envelope was addressed to Sasha's home address, which she'd found on the internet. The only reason she even had the post-office box number was because it turned out she was the lawyer for the theater group. She'd recognized the theater's unusual name, Darklander Mystical Mystery Theater, as one of her pro-bonos she undertook twice a year. The knowledge of that had knocked some of the wind out of her sails, but lately funny things had come her way. Take inheriting a mansion from her father. A father she had thought long dead.

Turned out he was only dead to her. He was none other than Sergey Gordievsky, a big Russian Mafia Boss. His will had stipulated all his wealth and possessions were to be left to her after finally discovering she was his daughter. Sergey was someone everyone knew by name and none by sight. Who knew he'd leave his only daughter a mansion and assets worth over thirty million dollars.

The house had at first terrified her, but with her friends' help and much wine and laughter later she was slowly acclimatizing to its size.

The added security measures her father had installed helped make her feel secure in the heart of downtown.

But all the money in the world did not take away the sting of what had happened to her last night. In the envelope was a letter outlining why she was suing the theater playhouse citing erroneous and misleading services rendered by her blind date. She was asking for two million dollars in compensation to cover her distraught emotional state. Tina was fairly certain it would yank the chain of her mystery man once he got blamed for the lawsuit. Really the amount of money she was asking for was ridiculously large but that was the point. She wanted them, specifically him, to squirm for a change.

"I know it's already four o'clock but can you courier this for me, Phil?" asked Tina.

Phil swiveled around in his seat, his streaked shoulder-length blond hair cascading around him. "Sure, not a problem, sweetie. Anything for you. Want me to add this to the account?" Flamboyantly he waved his pink manicured hands at her.

Tina was currently working on a case that involved Lieutenant Mitch Vlascenko who was up before the Court for misconduct. The actual incident happened two years ago but with how things worked in the slow motion movement of the Courts, his case was just now being heard.

"No. I'll cover this out of my own pocket."

She reached for her wallet. Phil placed a hand over hers. "Sweetie, that ain't necessary. Gary's our courier and he owes me big time."

Tina smiled for the first time that day. Phil was openly gay and Gary was his current lover. "Dare I ask what happened?"

"Sweetie, trust me you don't want to know. Those innocent ears of yours would be burning off you. Let's just say it's payback time."

"You are evil," teased Tina.

"No, he's evil...in that deadly good way that makes you shiver." Phil cocked an eyebrow up while slanting his eyes to the right.

Tina turned her head to check out who he was referring to and gulped. Walking through the Clerk's office door was none other than her client—Mitch Vlascenko.

She froze. Without thought she felt her psychic mind reaching out to his. A rush of warmth speared through her body, causing her heart to flutter erratically. She managed a peek into his thoughts—they were sensual, dark and mysterious; causing her breasts to swell and her nipples to pucker into tight buds. Then as if a door were closing he slammed shut his mind, the power of that one thrust sending a spike of righteous anger through her.

Tina always used her psychic powers to read her clients and it always helped her win those hard cases. Not so with Mitch. She couldn't read him.

A devilish grin, hard around the edges creased his chiseled face. Dark brown eyes reminding her of melting chocolate penetrated her with one deadly gaze. She felt her eyes closing as a rush of unknown desire to take him, claim him and bite him shook her rational mind. *Bite him! Ugh. That's gross.* Tina shook her head, feeling her long mane of hair swirl around her.

She prayed to god that she wouldn't resort to stuttering, a childish habit she had developed when she'd gotten teased at the private All Saints Catholic Academy her mother had insisted she attend.

"Take a deep breath," teased Phil, averting his head to pretend he was occupied with the computer.

"Stop that," she muttered.

"He likes you."

"Does not."

"Does so."

"Does not."

"Does not what?" asked Mitch, his tall, muscular frame shadowing her.

31

In the small confines of the Clerk's office, having Mitch's towering presence fill up the space made her recall that lovely warm invading feeling she'd tasted last night when her mystery man had loomed his hard, chiseled body over hers. Tina smoothed a hand down her side, realizing her latté was probably cold by now.

"Nothing. I'll meet you in the side office to go over your case." Tina felt her confidence soar. She'd managed to speak without stuttering and she'd sounded sure of herself. *Which is exactly what I am.*

He nodded without speaking and then turned and marched out the door. Her eyes were drawn to the casual stride of his long legs, which were sexy as hell.

"Nice ass," drawled Phil.

Tina wished he hadn't said that because that was exactly what she'd been thinking. *Buns of steel.* She eyed his leg movements in the dark navy formal police uniform he had to wear before the judge. Another mind-blowing rush of desire surged through her body, tingling all those hidden places the mystery man had worked at so expertly last night.

"You okay?" asked Phil.

Tina knew her face was flushed because of her racy thoughts. She wanted to shout at Phil, *Nope. Not right at all.* Instead, she cleared her head of the events of last night and forced herself to think of the case before her.

"I'll be fine."

"Watch yourself with that one. He's the type that smiles sweet and then devours his prey."

Another pink wave of embarrassment washed over Tina instantly. Thinking of Mitch devouring anything caused her womb to clench eagerly, making her teeth ache in a weird way that caused her to shout at Phil. "You're not helping."

Phil laughed. "Yes I am. It's about time you thought of what a man could and would do to you. Go for it, sweetie. I wish I could."

Go for it. That idea was as ludicrous as what had happened to her last night. There was no way she could seduce Mitch. He was hard core cop. The type that worked the night shift usually dealt with murderers on a nightly basis. Mitch seemed like the type of guy who could casually take it all in without letting his work affect him.

The notion of going for Mitch was startlingly erotic. *Can I do it? Hell yes.* After all she'd just fired off a law suit to demand satisfaction and it was about time she shook off that shy persona of hers.

Tina grinned as she opened the door to the side office knowing Mitch was waiting inside.

"Took you long enough," he snarled.

Her smile faded the instant his scent snared her. Whiskey, leather and Cuban cigars. Axe—that potent male body spray that caused a gush of hot, wet desire to thoroughly coat her panties with need. *What? Does every male wear that cologne now or what?*

"So, what do you think? Am I guilty as charged?" His voice rumbled low, vibrating all the fine hairs on her skin like a lover's caress.

Tina blinked while taking a chair as far as possible from where he sat. *I am so in trouble.* "I don't know, are you?"

Mitch shifted uncomfortably on the hard wooden chair. His frame was too large for the chair but they were designed that way on purpose to keep clients on edge.

"No. I would never hurt a woman." Mitch's voice was a husky seductive whisper of truth.

"I know," she replied.

"You do?"

Tina opened the case file she'd taken from the Clerk's office. "I've read the case and they don't have any substantial evidence. It's all she said, he said. Plus I know you wouldn't hurt a woman. You're not that type of cop."

He laughed, but not in a humorous type of way.

"Something I should know, Mitch, before I go into Court and plead your innocence? In case you missed it, I'm you're lawyer and I don't like surprises, so if you're hiding something you confess to me now or we'll both regret it later."

He leaned forward, bracing his large hands on his muscular thighs which stretched his dress pants. "No. I'm innocent of the charge, but Tina if you have dinner with me later tonight I'll let you in on a secret."

Dinner? With Mitch. Tina eased back in her chair, reaching for calm. She instinctively felt her mind pushing into his, seeking his true motivation. Like earlier, she met warmth and darkness—he remained closed to her.

This is exactly what she had been planning but he'd taken command of the situation before she could utter one foolish word. She waited a full two minutes before speaking.

"I...I...I—"

"Feel free to say no."

"No. I mean, that's not what I meant to say. Yes. Yes. I would love that."

"So would I." A sinister like smile creased his face which gave her a very uneasy feeling.

Tina stole another glance at Mitch, noting how he had the ability to transform himself within seconds from angelic to sinfully sexy and all male with a teasing smile, slant of his eyes and set of his chin. *Really, gentlemen are overrated.*

Chapter Four

Pleased with his not guilty verdict from the judge, Mitch was now furious. After asking Tina out on a date he'd gone to his desk only to get an email from one angry, frustrated Sasha, who had informed him Tina was launching a lawsuit for erroneous, misleading representation. Mitch didn't even know what that meant. *Just who the hell does she think she is? A fucking lawsuit!* All he knew was that so-called shy Tina really had balls. Big balls it would appear because she'd hired one of the city's top lawyers to represent her suit. *How the hell was she able to fire off a lawsuit so quickly?*

The email he'd received from Lance's sister had knocked him on his ass. A lawsuit. Because of him. Sasha had lit into him, telling him not to bother showing up tonight for the second night of bidding for the charity auction. Like that was going to happen. Mitch had told Sasha in no uncertain terms that he'd be there tonight with or without her consent. She'd huffed at him but had finally relented. He should have felt better with that one victory but he didn't.

So Tina wants to stake me? Well, after tonight she'd discover he wasn't a man to be toyed with. And he wasn't a man who cared at all for the word erroneous. *What the fuck does that mean, anyway?* Well, it didn't matter. After Mitch was done wining and dining Tina like the proper gentlemen he could be he was going to show her how fucking erroneous he really was. The urge to give into Lucifer's command and claim her sounded lovelier with every heart-pulsing minute.

Mitch's eyes narrowed as he played with the handcuffs looped to his belt. *Yeah, I'll give you misleading representation alright, Sweet-cakes. That's a promise.*

TINA WAS NERVOUS. SHE'D never been to Dimitri's Restaurant. It was one of the best restaurants in the city. Located on the top floor of the Sheraton Hotel, it provided a panoramic view of the city. She checked her watch for the third time. It was eight o'clock already. By the time Mitch showed up, if he did, they'd only have an hour for dinner because she had to meet up with Cindy and Nora for the second night of the theater's blind date charity auction. *Trust a cop to be late.*

Having ignored her phone for most of the day Tina had given in and taken a call from Cindy. Telling her friend what had happened last night actually made her feel better. Cindy of course had offered her usual condolences.

When Tina had coughed up she had fired off a lawsuit to the theater, Cindy had laughed non-stop, informing her she was wicked. Then when Tina confessed she'd accepted Mitch's dinner request Cindy had become very quiet. Sensing it was because of tonight's second night with the theater's blind date auction, Tina had quickly informed her friend that she wasn't backing out. As much as she longed to go all wild with Mitch he'd have to wait until later in the week. The three of them had committed themselves to the theater's auction and Tina would not disappoint her friends.

The gorgeous Greek bartender refilled her vodka cranberry drink. "A refill from that gentleman over there." He gave her a boyish grin.

Tina knew it was wrong to accept the drink because she was meeting Mitch but the bastard was late. So, what's a woman supposed to do? Say a polite no thank you. Normally, she'd do just that, but not tonight. Tonight she was looking for action and if she couldn't get that from Mitch maybe she could actually pick up a guy for once. A nervous giggle escaped. She swiveled her body on the tall barstool so she could politely smile and nod at the gentleman who'd bought her a drink.

The man was mid-thirties, had wavy blond hair and was by all standards good looking. Too bad her heart didn't go all aflutter. The man raised his glass up at her and then made as if to join her at the bar. At that exact moment, Mitch walked into the bar. In one smooth cop move he took in her posture on the barstool, the guy getting out of his chair and within a second he'd cased the joint—knowing exactly what she'd done.

A thrill of alarm raced through Tina even as her face flushed nervously. Mitch strolled toward the man who was now making his way toward her, stilling him with a hand to his shoulder. A minute later the man returned to his seat. Mitch's eyes never left hers.

"You terrified that guy," she said, when he joined her at the bar.

"Double rum and coke," ordered Mitch. Then he turned those chocolate brown eyes on her. "He deserved it. You're mine tonight. He's lucky I didn't kill him."

Tina swallowed. Her throat was parched for another sip of her drink but she was afraid to break the moment. She sensed Mitch was looking at her. Really looking at her, like she was a woman and not just the force's hired lawyer.

"This was a bad idea," she muttered, immediately trying to use her psychic ability to sense his intentions. Like the other times—nothing. A blank wall of darkness seeped into her body, heating her with its mysterious elusiveness.

His pale hand touched hers. Mind-numbing, toe-curling warmth spread through her entire body. She closed here eyes to savor the rush of sexual adrenaline that one touch ignited through her system.

"Maybe. But it's too late now."

Before Tina could respond, the head waiter told them their table was ready. Tina didn't want to take Mitch's offered hand but with the two vodka cranberries she'd absorbed on an empty stomach she was afraid she'd land on her butt attempting to climb off the tall barstool.

"Here, I've got you."

Large warm hands spanned her hips. Gently, he hauled her body off the stool so that they stood side by side. Her stomach muscles were fluttering like mad and it didn't have anything to do with the alcohol. She inhaled Mitch's scent—that male, locker room cologne, loving what it did to her senses and thoughts. Wicked, wicked thoughts. *Funny what male cologne can do to a woman's body.*

"I should apologize for being late. I'm sorry. I didn't mean to make you wait."

His voice was a low rumble, causing her nipples to ache with yearning.

"It's okay," she squeaked out.

"No, it's not. It won't happen again. A woman like you shouldn't have to wait," he said, emphatically.

Not sure what to say to that comment Tina allowed Mitch to lead the way. Silently, with only the heat of their bodies making her edgy they followed the waiter and a minute later they were escorted to a dark, secluded booth. Tina's heart leapt furiously in eager anticipation. She'd always wanted to be wined and dined by a sexy man and it looked like her wish was about to come true.

"Dare I ask how you arranged all this?" She was pleased the fluttery feeling in her stomach wasn't making her tongue-tied. Usually around cops she started to stutter. It was an old childish habit she had fought daily to overcome.

"You don't want to know." He took the seat directly opposite hers.

Instantly her bare legs brushed against his long legs. Mitch was dressed for the occasion. He wore black dress pants and a black dress shirt. No tie. That would have been too much to expect. He left the top two buttons on his dress shirt undone providing her with a tantalizing view of his dark chest hair. A hot memory of her mystery man's chest caused a flush of desire to spread like a wildfire across her face.

"Are you okay?" he asked.

If Tina could have died from embarrassment this was the moment. *Yeah, I'm great. Just can't get this sexy man from last night out of mind.* She giggled, instinctively placing her hand over her mouth.

"I love the sound of your laughter."

"Really?" A large grin spread across her face. *The guy likes my laugh. Will wonders never cease?* "It's too girly. People are always making fun of it."

"I bet those people are of the female persuasion."

She glanced at him. He was giving her a hot look. The blush on her face got a shade darker.

"Sorry, I've made you uncomfortable."

"No...I mean, yes...I mean, no..." Tina inhaled. "I'm not used to compliments. I like them, but I'm an easy blusher."

"I like a woman who blushes...I especially like it when that blush covers all of her soft, ivory-like skin."

"You're just saying that to make me uncomfortable, now. I'm on to you Mitch Vlascenko."

"Tina if you were on to me, we'd both know it." A devilish bad boy look caused Tina's juices to seep in earnest onto her panties. She knew it was her turn to retort but she was digesting the image of Mitch's large, masculine body on hers, those dark chest hairs of his teasing her nipples and for the life of her she couldn't think of anything to say.

"The devil got your tongue?" He leaned back in the booth, purposely brushing her legs with his. The intimate action stilled her thoughts while causing her heart to race and her cunt to clench with eager anticipation.

Luckily Tina was saved from saying anything because the waiter arrived with an assortment of Greek appetizers and a bottle of red wine. After that they settled into more polite, safe topics to talk about. Both of them however were keenly aware of the sex-driven energy coursing around them. After they'd both eaten their main courses, Mitch asked if they could have dessert to go, which thrilled her.

Not wanting to appear too eager and hopeful, Tina let Mitch help her into her evening coat as they both prepared for the outdoors. The weather was still warm so Tina had worn a short curvy black skirt which reached her knees, and a silver sequined off-the-shoulder top. The top had been a gift from Cindy who had insisted she have at least two sexy shirts in her closet. Most of what she wore consisted of casual dress pants or skirts and plain white dress shirts. Dressing up wasn't a requirement for the Courts. Dressing somewhat plain was a requirement when dealing with testosterone-fired cops on a daily basis. Instantly she was reminded that Mitch was the total male package. Hard around the edges but Tina was getting the sense there was a soft, compassionate part to him he tried hard to keep hidden. She also sensed there was an equally dark part of him buried deep within his psyche.

"My place or yours?" he asked the second they got in the elevator.

"I'm not sure..."

He silenced her so-called protest by flanking her body up against the elevator wall. Bending down, he cupped her face and kissed her. It wasn't a kiss that asked for permission. It was a kiss that took. Demanding. Controlling. A warning this was a man not to be trifled with. This was a man whose cock was hard for her and he was letting her know it. This was a man who wanted her.

A second later, Tina answered his probing tongue with her own. He was tall—a good six foot four of towering male strength. His height made it hard for her to wrap her arms around his wide frame, let alone get a feel of that silky brown hair of his she desperately wanted to stroke. *What is it with me and tall men?*

The minute he broke the kiss, nipping at her lower lip like he didn't really want to release her, she remembered her previous engagement. "I can't."

"Yeah, that's what I thought." His tone was edgy and clipped.

"No, it's not what you're thinking. I'd love to...really love to but I promised my friends that I'd meet up with them at this blind date charity auction."

He nodded but didn't say anything.

"Can I get a rain check?" She asked hopefully.

"When hell freezes over."

Mitch marched out of the elevator lightning fast before Tina realized what she'd wished for and wanted was now totally out of reach. She fought not to give into the angry tears threatening her control. Mitch had wanted her and she'd asked for a rain check. *What type of woman asks for a rain check? A bloody stupid one.* She wiped a tear that had slipped free and with determination took stock of her situation, realizing the night might not be a total loss as she checked her watch.

Calling her driver, she informed him where to pick her up and taking another calming breath she mastered her emotions. *I will have fun tonight, just you wait and see, Mitch. I'll show you.*

Chapter Five

"Took you long enough. Cindy and I were getting nervous you were going to be a no-show. So how did things go with Mitch?" asked Nora, toying with her strawberry daiquiri.

"Great."

"Oh, Tina..."

Tina took a seat next to her friends. The urge to tell them what had happened to her tonight was overwhelming. She longed to reveal to them how Mitch's kisses had unlocked that wild part of her and disclose how much she had wanted to go home with him and finally have that mind-blowing sex everyone talked about. However she was saved from spilling her sad tale when the lights dimmed for the second night in the theater's week-long blind date charity auction.

Settling back in her chair she took the offered drink Cindy had bought her, mouthing a thank you to her friend. The minute the men hit the stage not a whisper could be heard. Tonight was swim apparel night and the place was even more packed than last night. About one hundred women were crowded into the theater's hall each waiting with bated breath to bid on their blind date of the night. And once again all the men wore masks.

Watching the men stride across the stage Tina felt a dark, sensual stroke of thought touch her mind, almost a teasing intimate caress causing her nipples to harden. Scanning the stage she sucked her breath in sharply. There on stage was a man towering over the rest, bare-chested with just the right amount of crisp dark chest hairs, clad in a black Speedo that didn't leave much to the imagination. He wore the required Zorro-like mask and then it hit her. It was Mitch. Her Mitch. The cop who worked the night shift was the same mystery man who had done all those wickedly erotic things to her and the same man who had fled, leaving her blood pulsing and her pussy screaming and throbbing for more.

Incredulously, Tina watched him glide around the stage and then he caught her gaze—those chocolate-brown eyes of his claiming her with one mesmerizing glance. He boldly winked at her.

"I don't believe it," she seethed, recalling his harsh words from the elevator. Words that had almost erupted a flood of tears from her.

"Ladies, are you bidding tonight?"

Sasha's voice broke through Tina, causing her to gulp. She felt immediately guilty for firing off that stupid lawsuit.

"Look, I wanted to explain—"

Sasha placed a calming hand on Tina's shoulder. "Do not. They deserve what they get. I haven't had so much fun in years," chuckled Sasha. Tonight she wore a shockingly low-cut red gown, topped of course with her purple witch's hat. She looked shiny, mischievous and sexy.

Sasha looked around the room. "The ladies love your men but your men expect you to bid on them."

"Well, they can expect all they want. I'm out of here."

Tina noticed Nora's orange hair appeared to be standing on end. She watched her friend grab her sweater and storm away from the table before either Tina or Cindy could stop her.

Tina realized Sasha was still talking to Cindy and that her voice had taken on a strange sing-song quality that had Cindy tapping her fingers nervously. However Tina couldn't pry her eyes away from Mitch. Dark, potent desire coursed like a thundering rainstorm through her blood causing her to pant with need.

Realizing she wasn't paying any attention to Cindy and Sasha's conversation, a zap of electricity caused Tina to jump out of her seat.

"What the hell was that?" she asked Cindy, getting up from her chair just as her senses realized another electrical current of energy was coming her way.

"Nothing," snapped Cindy, running out of the hall without looking back.

Sasha's voice was crisp and clear. Turning toward Tina, she said, "That, Tina, was magic."

Tina laughed at the woman's ludicrous explanation, realizing she was probably still in her theatrical role. The sound caused all the men on the stage to stop walking. One male in particular growled a "back off" sound that awoke something primitive within Tina, making her teeth achy with an unusual urge to bite something. Preferably something warm and slightly salty.

"Let it happen. But right now if I were you I'd run."

Tina didn't need to totally understand what Sasha meant—the urge to flee slammed into her. The desire to get away from Mitch raced through her blood and this time she actually felt her legs moving swiftly through the hall without conscious thought. *Hell can freeze over buddy because I don't do second chances.*

An evil mocking laugh taunted her as she raced from the hall to her waiting limousine. The laugh should have warned Tina she was in way over her head when it came to Mitch but she ignored it.

"Home," snapped Tina the minute the car door shut and locked behind her.

Thirty minutes later she was pulling off her clothing in the safety of her large bedroom, tears streaming down her face.

"I hope those tears are for me."

His voice edged out of the dark confines of the corner of her room. She felt the lush caress of his voice like a warm breeze stealing over her skin and wished she hated him.

"How the hell did you get in here?"

"Hell likes me and it would appear that hell likes you a lot too."

Before Tina could digest his words, Mitch was on her, his frame forcing her hard up against the wall, his cock pressing with equally determined intent into her belly.

"You asked for this."

His mouth came down swiftly on the throbbing pulse at the base of her throat...his teeth biting deep, claiming her, taking her blood, draining her body, taking her soul and claiming her as his. His shaft felt like steel as it rubbed up against her belly. A hot surge of desire seeped out of Tina as her pussy muscles quivered. She was on the verge of climaxing.

The cold, dark knowledge that he was taking her unleashed the sexual creature hiding within her. Her nails raked into his back, holding him tight, forcing him to do it—bind all of her to him. Something weird was happening to her teeth. The edge of pain as her incisor teeth elongated caused her to shift her neck, making it easier for her to bite his offered throat. His gasp of delight unleashed tremors in her cunt that spiraled with heat throughout her entire body.

He ripped the shirt off her. She tore his shirt off. Naked, chests heaving together, she felt the moment when her true self awakened. Mitch licked her neck, sealing the bite with his special saliva. She did the same, tasting the coppery flavor of fresh blood. His blood. Framing her face with his large hands, he looked into her eyes. She saw sadness, felt his desire for her warring with something hidden, something locked down tight inside him.

"You are vampire?"

His words were hysterical. She laughed. He didn't.

"No, I'm not. I'm a psychic."

His heated gaze lowered to her now bare breasts, the nipples tight brown buds of wanting.

"You are wrong, Tina. I've tasted you. You've tasted me. Not only are you a vampire but your blood is pure. You are a *levista*...a born vampire."

She laughed again. Then his erotic words sliced through her mind, causing her eyes to bulge.

I want to taste all of you. I want my cock to slide into that deliciously tight cunt of yours and take you over and over again. I want my cum to slide down your throat. I want it all. I'm going to take you and you're going to let me and welcome my mastering of you.

The images. Her on her knees, ass in the air as Mitch's large frame pounded his thick cock deep inside of her; her legs, ankles crossed behind his head as he kept her arms pinned above her head so he could bring her orgasm after orgasm, caused that very thing to happen to Tina. His words, the burning images he was throwing into her mind, the deliciously wicked ways he was going to brand her as his caused Tina to have her third mind-shattering orgasm simply standing there with her mouth open in total astonishment.

"You are mine. And tonight I claim you. All of you. In every way, my little *levista*. Who knew following Lucifer's will for once is actually going to give me pleasure?"

Still trying to come to grips with Mitch's ability to send words and images into her mind, or the fact she'd just experienced an orgasm without anyone touching her, Tina couldn't react when Mitch's teeth scraped over the budded tips of her nipples.

"I want to fuck you hard and fast, but I'm not going to, Tina. I'm going to savor all of you, because I wouldn't want you to be left unsatisfied."

Tina sucked in her breath. Sasha had told him about her firing off the lawsuit. "Look Mitch, I only did that—"

His lips clamped down hard on her right nipple and his teeth bit into her, piercing her breast, making it impossible to speak. A euphoric feeling overcame her, as he moved her body from the wall to the bed, the entire time suckling small amounts of blood out of her. Her hand inched up to his thick, wavy brown hair, forcing him to keep at it. A swipe of his tongue sealed the small puncture wounds.

When Mitch raised his head a kernel of fear spiraled through Tina's body that was weeping for more of his touch. Gone were his sexy chocolate-brown eyes. Two devilishly-red pupils gleamed at her, hot with utter male possessiveness that said to hell with what she wanted.

He moved off the bed and stripped out of his jeans in record time. Tina's eyes got caught on his proud cock that was reaching, jutting out toward her. She licked her lips, wanting to taste him. Needing the feel of that cock deep within her. Then his large hot frame was once again covering all of her.

Take off the skirt and panties. I need to eat you.

It was a bristling command, pushed hard into her mind.

She instantly obeyed, knowing Mitch's tongue would deliver another soul-shattering orgasm to her already swollen cunt.

Bracing himself on his muscular arms, Mitch let her squirm out of her clothes. The minute she was totally naked, he scooted down her body, nipping her with love bites as he went. Each tender nip was followed by a light sealing lick from his tongue. He bluntly pushed his face between her legs, spreading her thighs, ensuring she was fully on display for him.

"Mine."

His possessive word staked through her body, heart and soul the minute his tongue gave her wet cunt a demanding, thorough lick. Lick, kiss, nip, another rough lick from his tongue to her pearled clit down her swollen pussy lips to the crack of her ass and back again. Over and over he repeated his ministrations until Tina was a thrashing wild woman on the bed, screaming over and over again for him to take her.

Not only was he demandingly playful with her cunt but he was sending erotic words and images once again into her mind.

Let the little levista *out to play.*

Tina didn't know what he meant but something dark, sinister and unnatural seemed to be taking over her mind and body once again. Instinctively she felt her mind attempt to shut it out but with Mitch's words and actions unleashing something wild within her she knew she was going to fail.

His teeth nipped her swollen achy clit, sending her spiraling into that lush liquid feeling. Mitch moved up her body, placing his throbbing cock at her entrance. With one smooth glide he shoved his wide cock into her unbelievably tight sheath. Tina's breath hitched. Searing pain at the invasion of his cock filling her froze her.

"Shit! I forgot you're a virgin."

The words were a ragged groan. Sweat had broken out on Mitch's brow, his eyes were now back to their melted chocolate look she much preferred and he looked shocked.

"Not for long."

Her hands were skimming up and down Mitch's back, loving the play of his muscles as they rippled from the tender caresses of her fingers.

When Mitch didn't move, Tina let herself breathe. Unbelievably she didn't feel any more pain, just a widening, a deep filling.

"Did you—?"

"No. Not yet. Tina...you don't understand, if I do this there is no turning back and you don't even know what you are. I can't..."

A crazed, wild invasion overtook Tina when understanding dawned. Mitch wasn't going to do it. His cock, already wedged deep, wasn't going to pierce her maidenhood. She felt him willing the hold, taking control of the beast that she felt living within him and she snapped.

She blinked hard, letting that wild thing encompass her and take hold of her reasoning.

"Oh hell."

That was the last coherent thing she heard a second before she totally lost it and let the demon within her awaken.

Chapter Six

The thick, coppery scent of warm, life-fulfilling blood swamped his senses, making him dizzy with the lust of her sex. She was decadent. She was the one and the damned part of him ached to give into the dark side of his nature and claim her. However, that's exactly what Lucifer wanted. And he'd be damned if he'd give the Master of hell this present.

"Don't even think it."

The husky, rasp of her voice caused his eyes to close—the deep, seductive rhythm of her words tugging at his mind.

"Do it."

Really, what other encouragement did any male need? With steely willpower he held himself still. The blunt end of his cock tickling the insides of her unbelievably tight sheath.

"I can't."

"Can't or won't?" She made a sensual movement with her hips, tilting and rounding them up, seeking to entrap his cock further into her warm cunt.

Edging further up on his braced arms, Mitch finally withdrew. "Won't."

Her head thrashed around on the white pillow, her coffee-colored hair falling in a wild array around her and she looked the picture of a sex goddess. Breathing deeply, Mitch ran a shaky hand through his tangled hair.

"Why? Why would you do this to me?" Gone was the demon voice as Tina's reasoning caught up with her body's demands. Sadly, Mitch liked the demon voice a little too much.

She deserves to know the truth. "Because that's what Lucifer wants me to do. Claim you. If I take your virginity you will be his."

A throaty laugh, tight with unshed tears caught him off guard.

"Lucifer? Seriously, you can't mean who I think you do?"

He nodded affirmatively. Her perky eyebrows drew together as she boldly assessed him.

"What does Lucifer have to do with you?"

The truth was startling even to Mitch's own ears. "Everything. I made a bargain more than a century ago that he could have my soul if he granted me immortality. He made me what I am today." Mitch flashed his large pointed fangs at her.

Sitting up, Tina didn't bother clutching the sheet to cover her nudity. Embracing the sexual side of her nature, she let him ogle her. "Lucifer made you a vampire, but you're saying I am one, and let me tell you he most certainly did not make me."

"No, he didn't. You're a born vampire. In my lifetime I've only encountered one other born vampire here in the human world. In the Darklander damned vampires like me are a dime a dozen. When I questioned Lucifer he said it sometimes happens, a genetic human anomaly."

"I don't understand half of what you said, but you actually believe this Lucifer person?"

"Look, I'm not human. I've been made a vampire thanks to Lucifer, who took my soul in exchange for giving me immortality. When I did that I ended up living for a century in the Darklander world where beings like myself, and others you couldn't even imagine, exist. A few years ago we were allowed to enter into the human world as long as we didn't reveal our true existence to humans. I'm not sure what the repercussions are now that I've told you all this but I'm not kidding. You are a born vampire."

Mitch paused and sucked in a breath. "When Lucifer tells you something, I've learned it's wise not to question him."

There was an odd, knowing twinkle to Tina's eyes that was starting to unsettle Mitch.

"He lied."

The statement hit Mitch square between the eyes, casting doubt to all he knew.

Clutching her to him wasn't the wisest of moves. The silky feel of her hot skin, the scent of her desire still fresh like dew on her arms traveled straight to his groin. "What do you know?"

"I don't know much, but if you humor me and allow me to call forth a friend of mine I'm sure we'll get the answers we both seek."

"Friend of yours? Is this a person I can trust?"

She looked down at her bare chest, her movement causing him to do the same. He gulped hard.

"Sort of. He's very selective and might not come if he knows you're here."

Mitch gripped her forearms tighter. "Your friend is a he. I don't think I'm going to like this."

"Well, it's the only way for us both to get some answers." She tilted her head up at him and gave a weak smile.

"Okay, do what you have to do, but I can't promise I'll be on my best behavior."

"When have you ever been on your best behavior?" A genuine smile flirted across her face. "Okay, you go hide in the closet and I'll call him."

"Closet? You're kidding, right?"

"Nope."

She gently pushed him off the bed. For a moment Mitch wondered what had happened. One minute he had the head of his cock wedged into her tight cunt and now he was being ushered into the closet. *This is not the best of nights for me.*

Allowing her to have her way, he sauntered butt naked to her closet. Only once the door was firmly closed, obscuring his view of her and the bedroom too, did he begin to question his sanity.

Using his vampire hearing he could barely hear what Tina was mumbling. None of what she was saying made any sense to him. She sounded like she was talking another language, but none he'd heard in his lifetime.

When the pungent smell of sulphur filled the small bedroom he burst through the closet doors.

"Get away from that!" Mitch pushed Tina away from the demon whose form was still coalescing.

She pushed him back, her strength momentarily catching him off-guard. "What are you doing?"

"What are you doing?"

Mitch longed to say more but the full presence of the demon took up the bedroom.

"You called, Mistress?"

"Frankie, I've told you before don't refer to me as Mistress. It makes me feel very old."

The demon bowed his blue human-looking head to acknowledge her. "Sorry. Do you want me to eat this creature for you?"

Frankie, who had morphed into a seven-foot male with bright blue skin and straight blond hair complete with two red horns on the top of his head, looked like he'd enjoy the prospect of eating Mitch. The demon's eyes glowed bright orange with glee.

"No. I called you forth to help us answer a few questions."

"Wait a sec, you called *him* forth?" Mitch knew he must have heard her wrong.

She nodded. "I told you I had to call forth someone...what's the big deal?"

"He's a big deal. He's a demon. I thought you meant you'd call a friend, or someone...not a demon. And how is it that you're even able to call forth one of Lucifer's pets?"

Frankie took a menacing step toward him. Mitch held his ground. Tina held up her arm, effectively halting the demon who now looked like he wanted to split him open and roast him over a fire, demon-style.

"Frankie has always been with me. He's my friend." Tina crossed her arms over her chest. Mitch was pleased to see she'd taken the time to get dressed before calling forth the said demon.

"Nice friend."

"Watch it, vampire man." The demon snarled at him. Mitch gagged. The demon's breath reeked of pickled eggs.

Tina waved her dainty hand in front of her face. "Frankie, what did I tell you? No pickled eggs. They don't agree with you. You're going to get heartburn."

Heartburn. Now that's a thought. Mitch fought not to grin. The easy banter Tina had with the demon eased the vampire living within him.

"Sorry. I couldn't resist," said Frankie sheepishly, casting his eyes to the floor.

"That's okay. I shouldn't have raised my voice at you." Tina walked toward Frankie and before Mitch could save her from becoming a demon-snack, she was hugging it.

"I don't have a lot of time. I'm supposed to be babysitting my brothers. What can I do for you, Tina?"

"Frankie, this man here is Mitch. He says about a century ago Lucifer made him into a vampire. He also claims that I'm a born vampire, which is really ridiculous. And he says that Lucifer wants him to claim me. I'm really not sure who else to turn to for answers but I was hoping you could help us." Tina said everything in her sweetest voice possible, just like she did when giving her summary before a judge. All innocence mixed with truthfulness, or how she viewed it.

"Tina, you're not going to like this. The human is partially correct," said Frankie.

"Partially correct?" Mitch knew he sounded like a parrot but the fact that Frankie was able to provide answers stunned him.

"Lucifer wants Tina because she is a born vampire, belonging to the oldest demon house before the turn of angels. If he claims you, he will have leverage on the house and use that to his advantage."

"See, I was right," declared Mitch, not sure what he meant by that.

"Goody for you. I'm totally lost. I can't be a real vampire. I can go out during the day and I'm not allergic to the sun or anything like that and I even go to church."

"So?" said Frankie.

"So, vampires can't do that."

"Says who?"

"Says everyone...all those books, you know."

Frankie raised an eyebrow at her.

"Actually, she's right. I can't go out during the day and crosses do burn me."

"Goody for you, human," mimicked Frankie.

Mitch edged forward. A hand on his arm stilled his advance.

"Stop it. That's not helping. I asked Frankie here for answers. Can you explain why he's allergic to the sun and I'm not?"

"Lucifer made him vampire-like, but he's not a true demon vampire. A true demon vampire is a superhuman. Do you know why you've always had me, Tina?"

The demon turned his orange-hued eyes to her. Tina shook her head.

"Each born vampire is assigned a guardian. I am yours. Your true parents were forced to give you up at birth, but I've been with you whenever you've needed me, even though we had to hide you in this cursed human world. I would be very careful with Lucifer. He's a true trickster. His link with this human enables him to control him."

Mitch shook off Tina's hand. "He most certainly does not control me."

"Yes he does. If you don't follow his commands what does he plan to do to you?"

Mitch seriously didn't want to answer that question. Tina's eyes gave him a sorrow-filled look. The last thing he wanted was her pity or for her to worry about him. Mitch gave a small shrug. "It's nothing. Don't worry about it."

"What will he do to you if you don't claim me?" asked Tina.

Mitch turned his eyes to the demon. "Why did you have to bring this up?"

"She needs to understand the consequences. This is her decision. I am only her guardian."

"Fine, then guard her. She doesn't need to know all the gory details." The minute Mitch said the word gory he knew he shouldn't have.

"Tell me. Everything." She placed her hands on her hips and slanted him a hard look. The lawyer she had trained to be was now at work.

"It's nothing."

"He'll probably make him into a human kabob for eternity just for fun, roasting him over the pits of hell," said Frankie.

A gasp tore itself from Tina's lips. "What can I do to save him?"

"Save me?" Mitch turned his attention back to Tina. "Sweet-cakes, in case you didn't notice, I'm already dead and damned...you can't save me." Mitch gave a sardonic laugh.

"Actually, she can."

"What?" asked Tina, swiveling her head back to Frankie. "What do I need to do and how?"

"Seriously, Tina don't believe what this demon says to you. You can't trust him, he's in league with Lucifer."

"I don't know where you get your far-fetched ideas, *human* but not all demons are Lucifer's underlings. My family is tied to the born vampires, we are free souls, free beings and nothing Lucifer does will ever entice us to join his ranks. That is not how we work."

Mitch wanted to argue the point but Tina was drawing Frankie's attention back to her.

"How can I save him?"

"You need to claim him and turn him."

"How?"

The demon smiled, baring his mouth full of double-rowed sharp canine teeth. Mitch shivered.

"Drain him of blood and then give him yours."

"Now, hold on a sec. I've been down that road before, demon, and no thanks."

"Hold him for me," demanded Tina in her no-nonsense lawyer voice, causing Mitch to shiver with dread.

At first Mitch wondered who exactly she was referring to but the minute Frankie's poker hot hands grasped his arms Mitch knew exactly what she intended.

"He's wrong! It won't work!"

"Do you promise me it will work?" Tina turned her eyes to her childhood friend who had been invisible to others most of her life. However, the minute she'd stepped into the mansion left to her by her father, Frankie had become a solid form. A solid demon but her true friend none the less.

Frankie smirked and nodded. "He might not like it much but yeah, it should do the trick. Can we hurry this up? Need I remind you that I'm supposed to be babysitting my three demon brothers? Trust me, the human world is not ready for them to be unleashed."

"Hold him tight."

"Don't do this, Tina. Don't! It's not worth it. I'm not worth it."

Tina took a deep breath sighing with what she hoped to accomplish. It sounded too weird to her. Learning Mitch's fate was tied to Lucifer's and that the overseer of hell was planning to torture him simply for not claiming her was too much of a burden for her sensitive soul to bear.

When Frankie had told her that if she could change him she'd free him from being Lucifer's slave that had sealed the deal for her.

Closing her eyes she gave herself up once again to that dark, controlling feeling she'd glimpsed a moment before Mitch's cock had invaded her tight opening. The rush of power soared through her cells, the knowledge of her true heritage—a pulsing thread of dark-light enabled her to hold on to the transformation taking place within her body. A flush of pain stole her breath as her fangs elongated. She felt her nails grow long and razor sharp, her eyesight electrifying everything within the room in hues of colors she had never seen before and her ears could discern the faintest of sounds. The true knowledge she was a demon vampire sank into her cells and with it came relief.

Her Russian mafia father was not dead. He too was a demon vampire like her. However, he had used his powers for control when he'd entered the human world. He was currently on the run from the Darklander police for using his powers but he'd managed to hunt down her true existence. And he cared for her. That knowledge was a bright spark in her mind. She felt the paternal link with him like warm blood oozing into her veins. When this mess with Mitch was sorted out Tina vowed to seek out her true father. Now, though, she had to concentrate.

Mitch was struggling to break free from Frankie's hold and that wouldn't do.

"It's now or never, Tina," said her long-time demon friend.

She nodded, moving closer, her tongue scraping over her sharp teeth. The scent of his blood clogged her mind. She knew one taste of him would be her undoing. He'd be pure male, potent.

"You need to drain him almost to the point of death."

"You moron, I'm dead already," snarled Mitch, wiging feebly now in Frankie's tight hold. "Call off your demon, Tina. Now!"

"I'm doing this for you, Mitch."

Frankie forcibly tilted Mitch's head to the side and pushed him to his knees. Mitch gave a muffled curse and then she moved in. Making sure he watched her sensual walk, she strode forward with all the confidence in the world when she felt none of it. Moving to her own knees she faced him, eye-to-eye. His pupils dilated with sexual awareness as she let her demon sex scent do its own job.

Her tongue gave a lick to his neck, digesting his nervous sweat and his growing excitement. She flicked her tongue again over the spot, causing him to moan. Tina moved to the large throbbing vein at his neck and then gave into the primitive urge to bite him. The first taste of his warm blood caused her cunt to spasm with need, her breasts to swell and her nipples to pucker hard. She fought the urge to rub her body shamelessly up against his. Instead she concentrated on sucking the blood out of him.

She knew the act should have shocked and repulsed her but it didn't. Giving into the demon vampire she was gave her the freedom and confidence she needed to save them both. *Or at least I hope so.*

"That's enough."

Dimly she heard a voice telling her to stop, but she didn't want to. The euphoric taste of his lifeforce was making her blood-drunk and she wanted more.

"Stop, Tina! You'll kill him for good."

Only when Frankie pushed at her shoulder did she truly hear his warning. With effort she released her hold on Mitch's neck, licking the bite wound with her tongue, allowing her vampire saliva to heal the two deep punctures.

"What do I do now?" Tina knew she was slurring her words. Her tongue felt thick and her body was sluggish; the urge to lie down and sleep pounded into her.

"You need to feed him your blood. Here, I'll help."

Frankie grasped her wrist and then before her sleepy eyes he ripped open the vein on her right wrist to forcibly hold it over Mitch's mouth.

Through cloudy eyes she watched her demon friend forcibly pry open Mitch's mouth to ensure her blood trickled down his throat. The minute Tina's blood reached his stomach, he awoke, grasping her wrist. His mouth clamped down hard. The pulling sensation of Mitch sucking her blood into his system was erotic enough for the tips of her nipples to harden even more.

"That's enough!" snapped Frankie, yanking her wrist from Mitch's mouth.

The demon kissed her wound and instantly the large gash healed.

"Now we wait."

"Wait? How long?" asked Tina, trying with all her might to keep upright.

"Sleep, Tina. I will keep watch."

"I thought you had to..."

"Babysit? Looks like I am," said Frankie.

Really, Tina knew she should stay awake for Mitch's sake but for the life of her she couldn't. She felt totally drained, exhausted with all she'd gone through in such a short amount of time that when she finally closed her eyes it was to sleep the sleep of demons. Dark, tranquil, blissful sleep—something she'd missed her entire life. Cocooned in silence, her body felt truly whole and powerful.

Chapter Seven

It was night three of the theater's blind date charity auction and none of them wanted to be there. Tina eyed her second drink, longing to gulp it down in a very unladylike fashion.

"I can't believe you dragged me here. I don't want to be here and you two resorted to blackmail to get me to come with you," whined Nora for the umpteenth time.

"Look, we don't want to be here either but those men need to be put in their places," said Cindy.

Tina noticed Cindy was going for a more business look tonight. She wore a blue no-nonsense dress suit that reached her knees, and she was all brisk business. Tina's senses sizzled every time she looked at her friend, Nora, who was burning up with a fever of righteous anger.

"I really don't think it's a good idea for me to be here. I'm not myself these days," said Nora, her voice a sultry purr.

"Trust me Nora, none of us are ourselves. By the way, I like what you did to your hair," said Tina.

"Thanks, but I didn't do anything to my hair, and what's wrong with your voice?"

"Then how did you get red, gold and brown streaks in your hair?" asked Cindy, diverting Nora's attention away from her, which was good, thought Tina.

"It's all natural, you like?" Nora gave a slightly terrified giggle.

Tina gulped down her drink, not caring that both her friends were watching her intently. "Nothing's wrong with my voice but there's something odd about yours, Nora." They were seated dead center so they'd have the best view of the men about to strut their stuff on stage tonight.

Why they kept coming to the theatre blind date auction mystified Tina. She longed to run out of the building, especially after what had happened last night, but she wasn't about to let her friends down. They were all in this together.

Nora leaned over to Tina. "Nothings wrong with my voice. Yours on the other hand sounds deeper, fuller," she gasped, "And much sexier."

"Sexier?" Tina tossed back a laugh. "I'll take that. By the way, your voice sounds like you're purring."

"What?" asked Nora, quickly adding, "That's insane...*pleeease*, people don't purr."

"You do," stated Cindy, who was ordering a drink from a passing waiter and asking if it was possible for a bowl of candies to be placed on their table.

The three of them were forced to stop their bickering when Sasha appeared at their side, clutching a bright pink witch's hat in one hand. She promptly placed it on Cindy's head.

"Thank you but I don't do hats." Cindy's words were a deadly zap of sarcasm.

"Ladies, I don't think you read the sign when you walked in. Tonight it's all about the magic. It's all about discovering your true potential, and letting the wild side out. That's why I called tonight, 'Your Magical Wild Fantasy Night.'"

"Ohh, that's original." Cindy popped a handful of colorful jellybeans the waiter had delivered to their table into her mouth.

"Hey, why does she get a bowl of jellybeans and we only get pretzels?" Cindy playfully swatted Nora's hand away when she attempted to steal a few for herself.

"She needs the sugar high, right Cindy?" said Sasha.

Sasha's perky black eyebrows drew together in a neat, whimsical way that had Tina wondering what was up. Tina noticed she kept adjusting her witch's hat, which matched the bright pink one Cindy had torn off her head.

"Look, aren't you supposed to be announcing the show? It's about to start," said Cindy.

Again, Tina thought Cindy's interruption sounded forced, like she was purposefully keeping Sasha from saying what she meant.

Gracefully, Sasha smiled. "Suits me. Let's get this show started." She turned and glided away. "See you later, gals."

Cindy shoved four more red jellybeans into her mouth.

"What did she mean by that?" asked Tina.

Cindy mumbled, "Nothing."

The stage lighting dimmed and then Sasha had the spotlight on her. "Ladies, tonight you're in for a special treat. Tonight each of my selected men will showcase their assets for you alone. Tonight each will strut their stuff and trust me, you won't be disappointed."

Tina fidgeted in her seat. "Alone."

"Assets," repeated Cindy, her mouth so full of jellybeans she couldn't cram another one in even if she wanted to.

"Special treat, my ass," snarled Nora.

The minute darkness settled on the crowd they all grew silent.

"Do you smell that?" asked Nora.

"Shh," said Tina.

"You all right, Nora?" asked Tina, sensing her friend's erratic heartbeat and lust that was now coursing through her mind and body as she avidly watched the man she called Hank strut his stuff on stage.

"Oh my god, he's stripping," laughed Tina.

"This is so good," drawled Cindy.

"This is not good at all," declared Nora.

"Where are you going?" asked Tina, watching Nora push back her chair to make her way to the stage.

"To kick some feline's butt," hissed Nora.

"What is she doing?" asked Cindy, moving her chair closer to Tina's.

"I have no idea, but I'm not going to interfere and neither should you."

Cindy popped more jellybeans into her mouth and mumbled she wouldn't dare. A few minutes later the curtain descended, and the stage lighting went black.

"Hey that's not fair. We didn't get to bid!" screamed a woman from the back.

"Hey, where did Nora go?" asked Tina.

"I have no idea, but isn't that your guy?"

Tina prayed it wasn't. If what Frankie warned her was so, than Mitch wasn't going to be the same. He needed to have his blood taken twice and that was her only goal tonight. Frankie hinted unless Mitch underwent what he did last night than Lucifer would still have a hold on him.

The hard part would be convincing him because true to Frankie's advice Mitch hadn't remembered much about what she'd done to him and he most certainly did not remember Frankie, her demon friend. Waking up in bed with him this morning had truly felt like a slice of heaven. And Tina wanted that. They just had to break his ties with Lucifer for good to grant him his freedom. Praying it could be done was what gave her the strength to watch Mitch follow Hank's striptease with one of his own.

"He's gorgeous."

Cindy's sentiment echoed her own. *Sinfully gorgeous, drop-dead sexy.* Hypnotized with his sensual actions and his slow skillful movements as he swayed his body to the seductive music, she couldn't help but gasp as he proceeded to unbutton his white tuxedo shirt.

Now I know how Nora felt. Tina's throat felt parched. After last night her demonic vampire senses were working in full swing. The overwhelming combined scents of blood left her feeling high. The urge for a small taste slammed like a cross through her. Pushing her hair out of her face, she resisted the urge to lick her lips. Instead, she concentrated with all her might on Mitch, looking for any signs of weakness. When none became apparent, she started to feel angry.

Why is he up there on stage stripping for everyone to see? A gasp flew from her outraged lips when he too yanked his Velcro tuxedo-like pants off, causing her eyes to glow red. Then the man, her vampire man, had the audacity to rub his hands over his crotch. Hoots of encouragement from the crowd urged him on. Shamelessly he worked his hands over his slick, oiled body. And it was oiled. Tina's heightened senses could almost taste the musky oil he'd coated his body in. She squirmed on her seat, her panties slick with her own cum, her nipples poking holes in the black off-the-shoulder top she wore.

"He's amazing. You're so lucky," said Cindy, reaching for more jellybeans.

"You keep eating those and you're going to get sick."

"Don't I wish. If only I could barf this curse away."

"What?" asked Tina, trying to pay attention to her friend but that was proving impossible. Mitch currently was tweaking his nipples much to the admiration of all the other women.

Cindy mumbled an incoherent answer and Tina knew why. A woman from a nearby table was climbing up onto the stage and Mitch couldn't have looked happier.

With skill that left her shaky with need, she watched him slide an arm around the woman's neck, bending her back. He flashed a sexy grin at the crowd but Tina caught the hint of his fangs lengthening. A demonic urge to ripe the woman to shreds overtook whatever common sense she had left. Mitch lowered his head to her neck, making sure she saw him give the woman's exposed vein a sexy lick. Gasps from the crowd as he, her vampire-man, swiveled his hips into the woman's ass, shattered Tina's remaining sanity.

Not caring that she was making a scene, Tina used her supernatural speed to make her way up onto the stage. Boldly she yanked the woman out of Mitch's hold, seconds before his teeth would have clamped down on her vein.

"I was hoping you'd save me." Mitch's grin rattled her to the core.

Tina let him draw her body to his, enjoying the cheer from the crowd as they assumed this was all part of the show. The minute his teeth clamped down hard, biting into the throbbing vein on her neck, she closed her eyes. Once again that euphoric rush of his taking her, claiming her, making her his, overtook the demon vampire she really was. Thankfully the black of the stage curtain shielded them.

Chapter Eight

The harsh clap applauding Mitch's forceful erotic sucking motion on her neck shivered into Tina's mind.

"Fuck," mumbled Mitch. His hot breath scaled the rash of goose bumps as he licked the puncture wounds clean, sealing them with his special saliva.

"I knew you could do it."

Mitch clutched Tina to him. "She's not for you."

"That's right, I'm not." Tina didn't need introductions. She knew without a doubt the apparition of the man laced with the taint of death, his feet inches from the ground, was none other than Lucifer. The god of hell.

"Says who? He has claimed you, as I commanded him to."

Lucifer's cocky voice wasn't sitting well with Tina. Wiggling free from Mitch's hold she turned, making sure she had Lucifer locked in her eyesight. "Actually I turned him." *Well, I plan to finish turning him once you leave.*

"What?" Both Mitch and Lucifer sounded incredulous. Then the god of hell laughed. It wasn't a pleasant sound. Painfully scratchy, like fingernails being raked down a chalkboard, it caused her to cringe.

Mitch took a step back from Tina. "What are you talking about?"

Crossing her arms for courage, Tina turned her eyes toward Mitch. Part of her was afraid to train all her vision on Mitch for fear of giving any leverage to Lucifer. However, she owed Mitch the truth. "Last night with my demon friend's help I turned you. I took your blood and then gave you mine." *And tonight once I do it again you will be free.* Tina longed to tell him that part but was afraid to disclose all her cards with Lucifer listening.

"You. Did. What?"

Lucifer's voice crashed into her mind, and for a second Tina faltered. If Mitch hadn't grabbed her she'd be lying on the cold concrete. They had made their way from the theater's hall to a secluded dark alley one block away. There was no safety to the night for Lucifer didn't abide by any clocks. He held the power of darkness and death to his command. That authoritative streak echoing in his voice was what completely shook Tina's confidence, making her second guess if she'd done the right thing.

"Do you have a hearing problem? I said I turned him."

"That's impossible," said Mitch. He pivoted his head toward Lucifer. "Isn't it?"

Lucifer didn't say anything. He simply fumed. His bald head with the large ink-black skull tattoo gleamed in the dark. His eyes turned red with fury. Tina knew exactly how he felt.

"What did you do to me?" Mitch's whiskey voice eased into Tina.

"I gave you another option."

"No, my child, you simply gave me another option."

The sadistic smile the broke across Lucifer's face was like looking at Hannibal Lector in the flesh. This time it was Tina asking the stupid question. "What do you mean?"

Mitch took a menacing step toward her. "He means because you converted me he can now convert me, instead of using you. Satisfied? Guess you really did manage to save your hide."

"That's not why I did it. I did it to save you."

"Well, thanks, but I told you before I'm already damned." The sarcastic, hurt laugh Mitch forced from his throat wasn't fooling anyone. He was mad. Angry she'd attempted to free him from Lucifer's hold.

Tina knew what she had to do. Focusing solely on Lucifer, she said, "I give you myself willingly but you must free him from your enslavement." Lucifer chuckled again. "And stop laughing. I can't stand it. Those are my terms. Myself, willingly but you must release Mitch for eternity. You will give him his life back and you won't ever tempt him again." She placed her hands on her hips, a pose she used when confronting an angry jury. This was her closing argument.

"I accept."

Lucifer's eyes flashed even redder. Fear traveled through Tina's gut like a hot poker. *What did I do?*

"No. I won't let you." Mitch's voice was cold and calculated.

"Too bad. The terms are set," declared Lucifer.

"Aye, they are."

The soothing melody that came from the sky crested through Tina, calming her erratic heartbeat, which had been laced with fear.

"Ahh, now, isn't this nice and cozy, the Archangel as our witness. Have you come to report to your boss or to the Mistress of the Darklander Council?"

"I report to only one boss as well you know. You know the rules, Lucifer. A willing sacrifice to save another grants both their freedom."

Is this our miracle? Tina looked up as the bright, yellow light morphed into a man. Tall, easily reaching six and a half feet, he was lean but steel muscles revealed themselves with ease. Long silver hair cascaded to fall in a straight sheen to his shoulders. He wore designer jeans and a white t-shirt with a neon yellow peace sign on it. He radiated angelic love and total command.

"I am Israfil, the Angel of Judgment." His heavenly voice was a hot tropical breeze, balmy and soothing to the soul. "By the heavenly decrees, from the laws of the holy virtues—"

"Shut up! I don't need you to recite the bloody virtues Israfil, in case you've forgotten I helped to write the soulless things," snapped Lucifer.

71

Tina moved closer to Mitch. He took her hand in his, cushioning her body to his. The heat of him settled into her, easing the unreal scene taking place.

"Then far be it from me, Lucifer, to remind you of the soul oaths. Willing sacrifices negate your hold. These two..."

Israfil held out his heavenly hands to indicate both Mitch and Tina. "These two are free souls, hands off to you, my fallen brother."

"Go fuck yourself." Red flames shot up from the ground absorbing Lucifer with those parting words he'd fired off at Israfil a moment before he vanished back to the pits of hell.

"Is it true?" Mitch's voice was slightly hopeful.

The angel nodded. "Go forth and live thy life with honor, Mitch. Tina, you are vampire-born but not soulless. Your selfless act to save Mitch's life has been inducted into the Book of Knowing."

Tina's eyebrows drew together in confusion.

"Ask your demon friend about the book, he will tell you all you need to know. My duty and judgment are final. Live this life to the fullest and love each other as two souls should."

In a wink of blinding, heavenly brilliance Israfil vanished, leaving just Mitch and Tina, holding on to each other in disbelief.

"Yes!"

Mitch's shout calmed Tina's nerves. The man actually jumped for joy, grabbing her arms to spin her around. This playful side of him warmed her heart.

"Let's celebrate."

"What did you have in mind?" asked Tina.

"Sex, what else," laughed Mitch, pulling her to him to unleash a fiery kiss that had Tina closing her eyes and seeing stars of pleasure.

His mouth took possession of hers and he wasn't to be swayed. Pushing her into the darker part of the alley, Tina's back was braced by the cool, grainy bricks of the apartment building. However, the feel of the rough bricks poking into her back wasn't what drew her attention or caused her nipples to beg for the feel of Mitch's tongue swirling over them. No. It was the tempting feel of his hard cock as it pushed against her belly. The only piece of fabric keeping Mitch's cock in place was the black tight sexy as all hell bikini briefs he wore.

Using her palms as leverage, Tina reluctantly tore her mouth away from Mitch's. Her hands slid teasingly slowly down his oiled chest, stopping at his nipples so her fingers could tweak and twist them, knowing how much he liked her ministrations. Before he could question her further she sank to her knees, kissing his shaft through the fabric with glee. Needing to taste him, she stripped him out of his briefs. His only answer was to close his eyes in ecstasy and groan a muffled curse of pleasure.

When his cock sprung free, it stood thick and proud before her. Her hands shook as they cradled his rod in her hands, eager to explore his length and the weighty sac that was begging for her fingers. She blew over the slit at the head, pleased to see Mitch rock back on his heels. Then her tongue darted out to taste his cum, which was seeping out of him. Potent, salty male. Tina moaned.

Since she had fully embraced her demonic-vampire senses every taste, scent and smell was magnified to the hundreds. Opening her mouth wide she stuffed Mitch's cock into her mouth, needing her teeth to scrape over his satiny, sensitive skin. He jerked, and she peeked up at him. His eyes glazed red in demonic-vampire purity, blazing at her with warmth and tenderness. She sucked hard; he drew a shuddered breath in.

"You're killing me." The rumble and seductive notes of his warm, whiskey-coated voice caused her panties to dampen with need. His nostrils flared, catching her sex, causing her womb to spasm greedily for the feel of his invading cock. Mitch grinned down at her, his intent clear. She read it in his eyes. He swiftly moved his cock out of her mouth, and his speedy hands skimmed over her flesh while he bunched her skirt up to her waist. He yanked down her panties without care, turning her to face the wall. He, her vampire man, was about to stake her to the wall.

Tina widened her stance. Using her arms for support she tilted her ass up, feeling the weight of her bunched up skirt at her waist. She knew her bottom gleamed white with his normal vision and that her cunt screamed red hot heat, something his vampire eyes would most certainly discern.

His hands reverently moved her long tresses off her neck. She shivered. The knowing of what he was about to do slammed like a pleasurable caress into her mind, senses and body. His teeth teased her nape causing her to instinctively angle her head more, laying bare for his fangs. Her own fangs had descended the second he'd cinched her skirt up to her waist.

In one skillful movement she felt taken. The width of his cock plunged deep into her cunt at the exact moment his fangs pierced her neck. He pumped and sucked. Long, thorough strokes told her she was his and he'd do what he wanted to her. He was claiming her, branding her and she loved it. Hues of bright orange and dazzling yellow danced across her eyes as the intensity of his taking her unleashed a mind-shattering orgasm that had her bucking her hips up to meet his dominating thrusts.

His hand gripped her mid-section, yanking her further up. He pumped into her in a fast ferocious way and then he tensed, his orgasm quickening through him while her pussy muscles milked his cock. He stilled, his cock still rigid inside her.

"I need to take you one other way." His voice was hoarse from passion spent.

Not trusting herself to speak, she allowed him to discard her clothing, not caring that someone could come into the alley. Naked, sex-coated skin to skin, he tugged her to his chest. A heartbeat later they were airborne.

The night's breeze caressed them in its own blanket of welcome. It finally dawned on Tina what exactly he meant about his other way. They were about to let their demonic-vampire senses suspend them in the air while they sexed up the night.

She giggled with that thought.

"Something funny?" Mitch tweaked her nipple and nipped her earlobe for good measure.

"Have you done it this way with anyone else?"

"No. But I've always wanted to." He glided them up past the clouds, the air slightly cooler.

Tina wasn't worried about the cold. Her demon friend told her she could regulate her own body temperature. With Mitch around she was sure she'd always be blazing hot within minutes.

His hands moved from her arms to cup her ass. She came alive with that one skimming of his hands.

"Put your legs around my waist."

Tina did as instructed. The minute she looped her legs and arms around him, he drove his cock back into her. They both moaned from the sheer beauty of it. Suspended, Mitch used his hips to thrust deeply into her and then he circled his hips which enabled his cock to hit an ultra-sensitive spot wedged deep within Tina's pussy. She cried out, the feeling shocking her. Mitch instantly repeated his movements until Tina felt as if she were crawling on top of him, desperate for that achy release as her entire body and mind tensed for the freefall of the orgasm, which was seconds away. When it came, she felt hot cum leak out of her. But Mitch wasn't done with her yet. Not by a longshot.

With his shaft still hard, he pulled out of her core. The expanse of heaven was awe inspiring as the stars lit up the sky. Without thought Tina was relying on her inner demonic-vampire abilities to suspend her limp, oversexed and totally satisfied body.

Mitch moved down her legs, licking her cunt clean, his rough tongue coming dangerously close to her sensitive clit.

"Put your arms above your head and don't move them."

She did as instructed. Her reward was Mitch's tongue going bull's-eye on her nub. He used his hands to spread her legs, forcing his wide shoulders into the vee of her thighs.

"I can't take any more, Mitch," Tina whimpered. Her body clenched as the aftershocks of her previous orgasms gave way to larger, more forceful crashes.

"Oh yes you can, and you will."

Damn he was right, she thought as an overload of sensations screamed through her once again. *This is pure delightful torture.* Mitch's tongue flicked super fast, patting her clit until she reeled back, yanking on his hair as the force of the orgasm caused her to falter out of her suspension. Lucky for her Mitch was there to catch her, moving off her quivering cunt to once again claim her mouth.

The musky ambrosia of her own orgasm teased Tina's lips. She answered Mitch's groan by staking her tongue down his throat. Using his suspension she pushed him down, making it appear as if he were lying on a cloud mattress. Then without words she leveraged her hips up and took his cock into her cunt.

"You going to ride me, Tina?" Mitch's hands were on her hips, the words an erotic promise of what she was about to do to him.

"Tilt your neck, Mitch." Her eyes flashed red, her teeth tingled with the need to taste his blood stealing her sanity.

"All fucking right," growled Mitch, turning his neck, wanting and waiting with bated breath for her bite.

Deliberately slowly she lowered her body onto his, ensuring his shaft remained deep within her cunt as her breasts molded into his chest hairs. Using one hand she tilted his neck more, his vein jumping eagerly to life. She scraped her fangs in an erotic caress across his neck and then drove them deep. His hips jerked up in response, his thick cock wedged to the tip of her womb. She sucked, tasting his life essence and without thought her hips moved up and down, riding him with vampire hunger. Sex and blood, two things she had only acclimatized to within a few days, were now an integral part of who she was.

"Tina, I'm gonna...aww, fuck," groaned Mitch, his fingers digging deep into her waist as he came, completely in time to her sucking motions on his neck. When he was finally spent, she licked the two puncture wounds to seal them. Her body, tired and well-satisfied, lay onto his, his beating heart matching her own.

"We're going to do that every night," said Mitch smugly.

"We are, are we?"

"Oh, yeah, that was totally amazing. You're amazing. I love you Tina but don't ever do that to me again."

She knew exactly what he was referring to. The fact she had voluntarily given her life to Lucifer still shook him.

"Trust me on that point, I won't."

"But we will, right?"

She crinkled her nose. "We will what?"

"Do that again and again and again, Sweet-cakes."

Tina grinned, feeling the weight of the night like a lover's reassuring caress. "That has to be the best closing argument I have ever heard. But I forgot to tell you something, Mitch."

He cocked an eyebrow at her. Tina's hands nervously slid through his silky hair.

"I actually lied to Lucifer. I didn't completely turn you. I need to take your blood one more time."

Mitch digested her words and then brought her fingers to his mouth to reverently kiss her knuckles.

"You can take all the blood you need, Sweet-cakes, as long as I get to make love to you over and over again."

Then Mitch laughed. Tina thought she had never heard anything more beautiful. His voice was filled with the promise of freedom and it was more powerful than the Archangel's words. Truly, everything was going to be fine. As long as they were together they could work things out. After all, they'd already met hell and were once again in the folds of the living.

Other Books by Renee Field:

Follow her on Facebook at https://www.facebook.com/ReneeFieldRomanceAuthor

Twitter @pararomance

Email: reneefieldauthor@gmail.com

Titan Series:

Rapture, Titan series Book 1

Bliss, Titan series Book 2

Romance Siren series:

Claiming the Temptress (novella) (HQN Spice Briefs)

Claiming Poseidon's Heart (mythology romance)

Claiming A Siren's Heart (mythology romance)

A Siren's Wish (mythology romance)

What to Read After FSOG: The Gemstone Collection (WTRAFSOG Book 7)

Witch Me Good (Sexy Salem Witch Stories Book 1)

Spice Me Up (contemporary romance)

Heart of Mind (paranormal romance)

Queen of Dragons (paranormal romance)

Fairy Cursed (Highlander, Fey romance)

Darklander Lovers Series (paranormal romance):

Be My Vampire Tonight (Darklander Lovers, Book One)

Be My Werecat Tonight (Darklander Lovers, Book Two)

Be My Warlock Tonight (Darklander Lovers, Book Three)

Warriors of Maida (mythology sexy romance series):

Love Me Wild, Book One

Love Me Tender, Book Two
Love Me Strong, Book Three
Contemporary Romance:
Embrace (sweet contemporary romance novella)
Summer Heat (new adult romance)

Don't miss out!

Visit the website below and you can sign up to receive emails whenever Renee Field publishes a new book. There's no charge and no obligation.

https://books2read.com/r/B-A-HRN-GNLR

BOOKS 2 READ

Connecting independent readers to independent writers.

Did you love *Be My Vampire Tonight*? Then you should read *Rapture*[1] by Renee Field!

[2]

Mermen aren't real. That's what biologist Jamie Winters thinks until a gorgeous Greek god enters her life and drowns her, forcing her to rapture into a Siren. Used to logic, she can't quite come to terms with Seth Cutter's magical undersea realm or the fact that he's a macho Titan.

Being a Siren causes Jamie's hormones to go into overdrive, which isn't good when she realizes that's exactly what Seth was hoping for. Sure, the sex is out of this world, but she's not about to change her character.

As Prince of the North Seas, Seth is used to having his commands followed. A decade of exile on land was easier than having to deal with

1. https://books2read.com/u/bMRq83

2. https://books2read.com/u/bMRq83

the sexy-as-sin Siren who tips the scales of his existence and doesn't listen to one word he says.

They must overcome their prejudices to recover stolen relics that are key to the undersea kingdom, stop a deadly plague and destroy an underwater diva who wants to rule the roost. Are they two souls destined for each other or will the Fates decide otherwise? Seth knows firsthand, Fate can be a bitch.

Read more at www.reneefield.com.

Also by Renee Field

A Warriors of Maida Novella
Love Me Wild
Love Me Tender
Love Me Strong
Love Me Wild

Darklander Lovers
Be My Warlock Tonight
Be My Vampire Tonight
Be My Werecat Tonight

Elemental Love
Heart of Mine

Riverton Cove series
Embrace

Titan series
Rapture
Bliss

Standalone
Claiming A Siren's Heart
Claiming Poseidon's Heart
A Siren's Wish
Fairy Cursed
Summer Heat
Queen of Dragons
Summer Heat
Electrify Me

Watch for more at www.reneefield.com.

About the Author

Renee loves to write a variety of genres. She writes for HQN Spice Briefs and also writes sensual paranormal romance, and contemporary romance as an Indie author. Field also writes nitty gritty young adult and paranormal young adult romance novels under the pen name Renee Pace. Renee calls Halifax, Nova Scotia, Canada home and loves her view of the Atlantic Ocean. She is a member of Romance Writers' of America, and her local Romance Writers of Atlantic Canada. She juggles work, four children and is a firm believer in soul-mates and the power of the sea.

Renee loves to hear from fans. She can be reached by email at reneefieldauthor@gmail.com

Read more at www.reneefield.com.

www.ingramcontent.com/pod-product-compliance
Lightning Source LLC
Chambersburg PA
CBHW020545130626
46552CB00007B/2756